Lightning Never Strikes Twice

Cynthia Hickey

DEDICATION

To all my loyal readers. I appreciate you.

Chapter One

One more room to clean, the boss's office, and Alisa Gosling could put the long, work-burdened day behind her. She'd taken on way too many jobs in her quest to own a house of her own. Somewhere away from the city. Somewhere perfect like a small town.

Alisa adjusted the earbuds as she listened to sea shanties and reached for the business owner's door. Opening it, she flicked on the light. The place looked clean, other than an overflowing trashcan. Still, she'd dust and polish it. She couldn't afford to lose her largest client.

After she finished dusting and her playlist looped back to the beginning, she reached for the trashcan. Several pages fell to the floor, joining an errant piece under the desk. Alisa dropped to her knees and reached as far as she could. Aha. Her fingers closed around the wayward pages.

She glanced down at the paper on top. It was a torn-up letter. Not handwritten but typed. If she hadn't spotted the words *corrupt* and *police*, she would've tossed the pages. Instead, her curiosity piqued, and she lay the sheets on the desktop and put them in order.

Ice water trickled down her spine. The letter was a threat, exposing Mr. Barker, the construction business owner, of cutting corners and padding pockets. The sender went so far as to accuse Mr. Barker of bribing city officials and the police to look the other way. The writer promised to expose the entire thing.

A beep sounded, signaling someone exiting the elevator.

Alisa shoved the pages in her pocket, locked the office door, and scurried under the desk. She peered out, her heart in her throat.

A man's shadow paused in front of the door. She could see his cupped hands around his eyes as he peeked through the frosted glass.

Alisa held her breath. Her cleaning cart sat right outside the door. Whoever was out there would know she was in the office.

The door handle rattled.

Alisa gasped.

A key clicked in the lock.

Another voice from someone she couldn't see called the man away from the door.

After several tense minutes, Alisa crawled from under the desk, the papers in her pocket crinkling. She'd turn them over to the police the first chance she had.

Stuffing the rest of the garbage in her cart and putting a fresh plastic bag in the can, she took another long look around the room. In her haste to hide, she'd forgotten to turn off the lights. Whoever had stood on the other side of the door knew someone was in the room. Who other than the cleaning lady after hours?

She unlocked and opened the door. After peering up

and down the hallway, she pushed her cart out. In an attempt to look innocent in case someone saw her, Alisa strolled nonchalantly toward the elevator, singing along with the song coming through her earbuds.

Outside the elevator on the first floor, two men, one of them Mr. Barker, stood near the reception desk in muffled conversation. Alisa smiled and kept on walking, hoping they couldn't hear how hard her heart beat.

Did one of them just call out to her? She wheeled her cart into the supply closet and grabbed the bags of garbage along with the supplies she carried back and forth. Without looking back, she kept singing and hurried out the back to the dumpster and her car.

Her hands started trembling so violently she could barely turn the key in the ignition. She backed from the space and sped away from the building. A glance in the rearview mirror showed Mr. Barker and the other man standing there watching as she drove away.

Why would someone be stupid enough not to shred such an incriminating document? Had Mr. Barker realized it hadn't been done and came back to make sure it had? Or was she jumping to conclusions?

A man as wealthy as Mr. Barker was sure to have enemies. People who accused him of all sorts of things. Maybe that's why he hadn't shredded the letter. He hadn't felt as if he needed to. Then why show up at the office well after eight p.m.? If he had more work to do, wouldn't he have simply stayed late?

She gave herself a mental shake as she pressed the garage door remote on the visor of her SUV and pulled in. As the door lowered behind her, she released the breath she'd been holding. Her shaky hands were the result of having read too many mystery novels. A business owner could show up at his business any time he wanted.

She set her purse and car keys on the kitchen island, poured herself a glass of sweet, sparkling wine, and settled in front of the television—her nightly ritual in order to wind down after a long day.

A news reporter stood in front of Barker Construction. Alisa turned up the volume in time to hear that a woman had been found dead and stuffed in a closet.

The hand holding her wine started shaking again. The woman turned out to be Mr. Barker's secretary. They weren't saying how she died, but the fact Mr. Barker had found her in a closet signified it hadn't been pleasant. As if murder ever was. And Alisa would bet her favorite pair of shoes the woman had been murdered.

Alisa couldn't wait until morning to turn over the letter to the authorities. She reached for her phone and called the police department who promised to send an officer over right away. Again, she put the pieces together on her kitchen table and snapped a photo with her phone. Just in case. When she wasn't pacing, Alisa peeked repeatedly through the blinds for someone to show up. Hopefully, the police and not someone who suspected she had the letter.

Relief swept through her like a burst of air when a van pulled in front of the apartment she rented, and a uniformed officer climbed out. She should never have taken the letter. Stupid.

A few moments later, a knock sounded at the door. Alisa opened it and ushered the officer in before locking the door again. "It's in pieces, but here it is."

He raised his eyebrows. "You say you found this in

the garbage? Are you in the habit of digging through the trash bins of your clients?"

"No. I noticed it when a couple of the pages slipped out of the overflowing can and fell under the desk. I'd really convinced myself it meant nothing until watching the news tonight."

"Why would that matter?"

"Because a woman was killed either while I was cleaning—"

"Wouldn't you have heard something?"

She shook her head. "I wear earbuds and listen to music while I clean, so I never hear anything."

Why did she get the impression his shoulders relaxed at her response?

"I'm sure it's nothing, Miss Gosling. Thank you for bringing it to our attention." He nodded and helped himself out.

Peering through the blinds again, she watched him slide into his van.

The officer hadn't shown his badge, and now he stared through the windshield at her apartment. The streetlamp cast a shadow on his features. The part Alisa could see sent spiders along her skin. She let the blinds fall back into place.

The next day, that same dark blue van appeared in front of every house she cleaned. Surely, that wasn't coincidence.

Instinct told her she'd stumbled across something dangerous. That it was time to run as far from Westport as she could go. Rather than go to her last job, she headed home, taking care not to act suspicious. As per her routine, she pulled into the garage. Inside the house, she turned on the television which would flicker through the blinds.

Then, she turned on her laptop and searched for a sanctuary. A town called Misty Hollow sounded like just the place. Cradled in a valley, the town was surrounded by miles and miles of wooded forest. She found a small two-bedroom house for rent on some ranchland and jotted down the address. Alisa erased her browser history and slid her laptop into its bag. Then, she emptied her cabinets of all dry food and bottled water before heading to her room to pack.

How would she leave without being followed? She hurried to the front window. No sign of the blue van. All the cars out front belonged to her neighbors. So far so good. Maybe they'd decided she wasn't a threat after all. It didn't matter. Alisa wasn't sticking around to find out.

Behind the protection of the closed garage door, she loaded her vehicle with as many personal belongings as would fit, grateful for a large-model automobile. When she'd packed in as much as she could, she did a final run through of the apartment, filled a thermos with coffee, and then slipped into the driver's seat.

Alisa backed away from the house she'd rented for five years and sped toward the interstate. She cast many looks in her rearview mirror but didn't see anyone following her. Of course, she wouldn't unless they were obvious. She wasn't a detective in any sense of the word.

Thank goodness for the coffee. She didn't cross over the Misty Mountain into Misty Hollows until the sun started to peek over the top. Alisa glanced at her GPS and drove slowly through the quaint little town, making note of the store signs, then continued down a country road. Five miles from town, she turned right onto a dirt road that passed under an arched sign announcing

Leaning O Ranch and stopped in front of a sprawling ranch-style house. She'd arrived.

Alisa yawned and plodded onto the porch then rapped on the front door. A dog barked inside. A sleepy voice told it to hush.

A few seconds later, a man wearing plaid lounge pants and nothing else opened the door. A large mixed-breed dog with a brindle coat peered around his leg. "Yeah?" the man said.

Alisa cleared her throat. "I'd like to rent the house you listed online."

He blinked rapidly, then ran his hand through hair kissed with auburn on the ends. The bluest eyes she'd ever seen narrowed. "Why didn't you call first?"

"I was on the road." She tilted her head. "Is it available? I clean houses for a living. I could clean yours for a break in the rent. Either way, I'm here and need a place to stay."

He rubbed his hands briskly down his face. "The cabin is available. It's out back and unlocked. Can we talk about this once I've had a chance to wake up?"

"Of course." Alisa smiled. "I'll unload my bags. Thank you." Her steps perked up on the way to her SUV. She had a place to stay. The ad had said fully furnished, so as long as things were serviceable, they'd do just fine. She wasn't picky.

The house with white aluminum siding looked like something out of a magazine, inside and out. Inside, it had been decorated with blues and yellows. Clearly a woman had lived here at one time.

The master bedroom contained a queen-sized poster bed. The hours of driving and the stress of looking over her shoulder made her tired. Alisa lay on top of the quilt and fell asleep.

~

"Well, find her! Search every small town near here, then branch out to the surrounding states. She's a woman alone and wouldn't have gone far." He slammed the phone down, cracking the screen protector. The woman was only a cleaning lady. How smart could she be? He ought to have Barker killed along with his secretary. Stupid woman. Didn't she understand what a shredder was for?

If news got out about this, he'd be ruined. They had to find that cleaning lady.

Chapter Two

Liam O'Ryan filled a cup with coffee and headed onto the back deck as he did every morning, rain or shine, hot or cold. The view of his land, the pond in the distance, the mountain towering over it all kept him at peace.

The door to the cottage hung open. So was the back of the SUV. "Come on, Buddy. Let's go see whether our tenant needs a helping hand."

Buddy bounded alongside him as he went down the steps and across the lawn to the house his mother had once lived in. After Liam's father died, she didn't have the heart to live in the big house without him, so Liam had built the smaller one for her. After her death two years ago, he'd rented it out. But never to anyone who simply showed up on his doorstep. That was a first.

"Hello? It's your landlord, Liam O'Ryan." When no answer came, he entered the house. "Ma'am?"

He found her asleep on the bed, curled up, hands tucked under the pillow that cradled her head. Soft snores came from slightly parted lips. Her hair, the color of the coffee in his hand, lay spread across the pillow. *What's your story, strange lady?*

Brown eyes flickered open, then widened. Before

Liam could react, she smashed the table lamp against his head, dropping him to his knees and spilling hot coffee down the front of him.

"No, Buddy," he ground through his teeth as the dog snarled. He glared at the woman on the bed, plucking his shirt away from his skin. "I don't think I'll rent to you after all." Liam put a hand to his head, relieved not to discover blood.

"I'm so sorry. You startled me. I acted completely on reflex." She scrambled from the bed, crunching glass under her feet. "I'll replace the lamp, I promise. Where's the broom?" She darted from the room.

Definitely the strangest person he'd ever met. With a groan, Liam pushed to his feet, ordering his dog to stay away from the glass.

"Here we go." The woman started sweeping the shattered lightbulb into the dustpan, then picked up the broken pieces of the lamp's base. "My name is Alisa Gosling. I'm not usually this frazzled. Well, maybe I am, but…anyway." She held out the dustpan.

Not knowing what else to do, he took it from her and headed to the garbage can in the kitchen.

"Please, I need this house."

He turned and stared into her pleading brown eyes, the same shade as her hair.

"I'll be working most of the time, just as soon as I find clients. There must be plenty of people and businesses who need a cleaning lady. I'll clean that big house of yours for two hundred off the rent. How much is the rent anyway? Six, seven hundred?"

Liam rubbed the back of his neck and glanced at Buddy. The dog's ears perked up as if to ask whether they could handle someone who talked so much. Liam wasn't sure. He liked the quiet, peaceful routine of running a horse ranch, although he could use help with the house.

"Okay. I'm Liam O'Ryan. Come to the house when you're ready, and you can sign the lease. Need help unloading?"

She shook her head, a smile gracing her pretty face. "No, thank you."

He gave a nod, then marched to the main house to change his clothes. "I hope we don't regret this, Buddy."

The dog woofed low in his throat.

"Yeah, you're probably right." They'd come to regret renting to her. His gut said so, his dog said so, and his dog and gut were rarely wrong.

After changing, he headed to the barn to muck out the stalls. His father had once run a large horse ranch. Liam preferred to keep his herd small and rent his extra stalls out to local horse owners who might not have the property on which to keep their horse. Plus, he'd branched out to a few head of cattle and some pigs and goats. More of a farm now than a ranch, and he loved every bit of it. Even the noisy, dirty chickens. Problem was, he didn't make the same profit his father had.

Liam glanced toward the house to see Alisa carrying a large duffel bag inside, then frowned. "Did she seem overly friendly?"

Buddy huffed.

"Yeah, I thought so too. A bit…eager." He shrugged and threw open the double-barn doors. Whatever brought her to Misty Hollow would show itself soon enough. Liam rubbed his head again, thankful the lamp she'd bashed him with had been a cheap one and not one of the heavier crystal ones his mother had left in the big house.

That would have knocked him out cold.

He cast one more glance to where the woman stood staring at the road. When a flatbed truck pulled up to the barn, she ducked into the house.

~

Alisa couldn't believe she'd broken a lamp against her landlord's head. She'd expected some cursing, anger—something other than confusion. Then, when she'd babbled on like an idiot, he'd simply stared at her as if she had a third eye. She was lucky he'd agreed to rent to her.

While she planned on cleaning houses, Alisa didn't want to live in town. Being in the country seemed safer somehow, despite several ranch hands milling about the place. But, they'd been here before her, so they couldn't have followed her from Westport. Everything would be fine.

Now, a big truck full of hay had pulled up, and she'd run like a frightened rabbit. No one knew her here. No one knew where she'd gone. No one would think of looking for her here. Time to stop running and forget what she'd found. Otherwise, the worry would drive her nuts.

Alisa put on her headphones and decided to ignore the men by the barn while she unpacked. She was a renter. Renters didn't meddle in the lives of their landlords. She'd sign the lease, clean his house, and mind her own business.

The top priority of the day was to print out fliers. She hooked her laptop to the printer she'd set up in the second bedroom and printed off the same fliers she'd used in Westport. When she had an armful, she headed into town. Since Liam looked busy as she drove past the barn, she'd sign the lease later.

Alisa made Lucy's diner her first stop, amazed at how busy the place was at the noon hour. When the hostess greeted her, she asked to speak to the owner. A few minutes later, a middle-aged woman with hair the color of a pineapple greeted her.

"I'm Lucy. You must be new to town."

"Yes, ma'am. I'm wondering if you'd allow me to tape one of my fliers in your window." She handed Lucy one of the printed sheets.

She glanced at it and nodded. "You aren't bringing trouble with you, are you?"

"That's a strange question."

She gave a one-shouldered shrug. "Every time a pretty young woman comes to town, someone dies. Sure, you can tape it in the window. I'm certain most of the shops up and down Main Street will let you."

"Thank you." Alisa ordered a BLT and diet soda to go, saying she'd come back to pick up her order and headed to the drugstore.

The back of her neck prickled as if someone watched her. Every time she glanced over her shoulder, no one seemed to be paying her any undue attention. Women strolled the sidewalk peeking in windows or entering shops. Several people came and went from the coffeeshop. So why did she feel as if someone followed her? Her imagination or something more?

Alisa shook off the feeling. There was no way anyone could have followed her from Westport. She wasn't that important. The police had the letter, and she'd told no one what she'd seen. There was no reason to let it bother her. Then why did her heart keep giving an extra little jump?

After she'd distributed all the fliers and picked up her sandwich, she headed for a picnic table under a large tree near the lake just outside of town. A gentle breeze blew over the lake, whispering through the tree branches.

Surely the woman at the diner was wrong. This beautiful, sleepy little town seemed like something out of a Hallmark movie.

While she ate, she looked up news articles on the town. One or two crime sprees a year did not make the town dangerous in her opinion. Westport had murders every day. Drive-by shootings. Break-ins. Besides, lightning rarely struck twice. No reason to think she'd been followed.

Sandwich eaten, she returned to the ranch. Liam exited the barn, leading a horse by the bridle into a nearby corral. She parked in front of her house and followed, leaning against the fence. Alisa hadn't ridden in a very long time, and she missed it. Maybe he'd let her ride once in a while.

Her landlord was too handsome for words. She couldn't decide if the tousled version from earlier that morning who'd worn nothing but lounge pants was sexier or the one in front of her wearing faded jeans that fit just right and a tee-shirt that showed his sculpted arms. It had been so long since Alisa had time to be interested in a man that she'd rarely noticed them. Cleaning houses and businesses after hours was a solitary job.

"We can sign the lease when I finish here," he called out.

"No rush. What are you doing?"

"Training."

That didn't tell her much. Alisa leaned her chin on

folded arms and continued watching. The stress of the previous day drifted away with the sound of cackling chickens and snorting pigs. She'd made the right decision coming there.

She wasn't sure how long Liam trained the horse, but when he exited the corral, leaving the horse to graze, Alisa found herself reluctant to leave.

He motioned his head toward the main house, leaving her to follow. The dog that had wanted to take her head off when she'd hit his master trotted by her side, his dark eyes returning to her every few seconds.

"Will he bite me?"

"Not unless I tell him to." Liam held the door open for her. "Or you try to harm me."

She sighed. "Again, I'm sorry. It was reflex."

"Not many people resort to violence immediately upon waking." He led her through the kitchen to the table where papers and a pen waited. "What brings you to Misty Hollow?" He tilted his head. "Lately, only those who are running from something come to our town. We aren't exactly on the main interstate."

"Um, a new start?"

"Are you asking me?" His brows lowered.

"No. That's why I'm here. Wanted something different." She could tell from the look on his face he didn't believe her.

"I'm charging you five hundred, which includes utilities." He motioned to the papers. "And, you keep my house clean. It doesn't get very dirty with just me and Buddy, but it does need the occasional dusting. How do you feel about free rent?"

"What's that?" It sounded too good to be true. Not paying rent would get her that much closer to owning her own home.

"My cook quit. If you cook for me and my men, breakfast and supper, and take care of the house, I'll give you free rent. If you can cook, that is."

"Not a problem. I'm a good cook." She grinned and picked up the pen, glad he'd changed the subject as he handed her a new lease.

If he knew she'd spooked easily, he'd run her off. Alisa couldn't let that happen. To avoid possible danger, she needed to stay put and blend in.

Chapter Three

After several nights of watching the state news and hearing nothing further about Barker Construction or anyone affiliated with the company dying, Alisa started to relax. It was quite possible she'd overreacted and relocated for no good reason.

But, she liked the small-town atmosphere of Misty Hollow and had three clients already, not counting her landlord. Not enough to pay her bills, but she had some money saved to tide her over. The free rent was the best part. She loved her little house.

First thing that morning was to transfer from her old bank account into the Misty Hollow branch. Then, she'd clean for her first client, an elderly woman in a gorgeous two-story that had to be at least one hundred years old. She couldn't wait to see the inside.

Alisa returned the nod Liam gave her as he carried a coil of rope to the barn. She'd need to clean his house that day. When she returned from town, she'd ask him when would be a good time—meaning when he'd be out.

Mrs. Mayfield, the widow in the house Alisa already loved, opened the door before Alisa reached the porch. "I've made coffee and cookies."

Ah. She would be a companion as well as

housecleaner. "Good morning. That sounds lovely." Alisa placed her cleaning supplies in the foyer and followed the elderly woman to the kitchen.

"When you're ready, dear, just clean the downstairs. I never go upstairs anymore. These old knees grumble when I do. I've turned the formal dining room into my bedroom, and I prefer eating in the kitchen."

Alisa glanced at the lovely staircase. Maybe she could still take a look around later. She glanced around the old-fashioned furnishings, crocheted doilies covering every chair arm. It reminded her of her own grandmother's apartment in the city.

"How are you enjoying our town?" Mrs. Mayfield set a cup and saucer in front of her. "There's cream and sugar on the table." She motioned to the dishes sitting next to a plate of oatmeal cookies. "I made oatmeal so it would seem more like breakfast." The woman laughed and sat across from Alisa.

"I love this town. The people are friendly." She added cream and sugar.

"Good thing you weren't here in the fall. Mm-hmm. Of course, the killer preferred blondes, but that was a time, I kid you not." She tsked.

"Killer?" Alisa's hand trembled.

"Serial killer." the woman lowered her voice as if there was someone to overhear. "One of our local police officers. The sheriff was fit to be tied, let me tell you. It was a bad thing for sure. Then, the year before, we had a young lady come to town with a stalker on her heels. Turned out the poor man had a brain tumor. Very sad. Oh, we've seen our fair share of trouble. What's your story?" She tilted her head, taking a bite from one of the cookies.

"Just looking for a place to settle down, buy a house…" She reached for a cookie. "I had nothing to keep me in the city and wanted something different."

"Some folks are starting to think Misty Hollow is cursed. This town was founded by good, God-fearing people back in the 1800s, but evil has seeped in."

Alisa shuddered. "There's evil everywhere, Mrs. Mayfield."

"That, my dear, is true. So, what do you think about the handsome, Mr. O'Ryan?" She waggled her thin eyebrows.

"He's very…quiet."

"The strong silent types are the best kind of men, sweetie. You should set your cap for him."

Alisa bit back a laugh. "Let me get settled in before thinking about relationships." She rose to her feet. "I'd best get to cleaning. I've other places to do when I finish here." She glanced upwards.

"Feel free to look around. I see that you want to. I'll be in the living room watching television. Just clean around me as if I'm not here."

The house had been everything Alisa had thought. Like a step back in time. Now, she stood in line at the bank waiting for a manager—well, the only manager— to finish helping someone else.

"Thank you for your patience. I'm the manager, Mr. Kingsley." A man in a business suit approached her. "You're wanting to transfer your funds from another branch?"

"Yes, sir. From Westport."

"That will not be a problem. Follow me." He led her to a glass-offed cubicle. "All I need is your identification and account number."

His eyes widened as he glanced at her driver's license. He fixed a stare on her, then turned to the computer. A few minutes later, he said everything had been done and welcomed her to Misty Hollow.

The whole encounter seemed a bit chilly. Not at all as friendly as she'd been treated by other town residents. In fact, the bank manager seemed surprised by her name.

Alisa shook off the thought. Here she was being paranoid again. The only way anyone would know where she lived now was by knowing her name and account number. Her blood chilled. She didn't have the mind of a criminal. Didn't think about what ifs. She lived a simple life. Now, she might have made a dangerous mistake. One she couldn't escape unless she ran again. No. If trouble came, she'd face it then.

~

Liam watched as a pale-faced Alisa carried cleaning supplies into the house. He motioned for his hired hand, Willy, to take over training the horse, told him to pick him up in town in half an hour, then followed her.

She leaned against the counter, taking deep breaths. "You all right?"

She yelped and whirled. "You scared me. Again."

"Not my intention." He narrowed his eyes. "You okay?"

"I'm fine. When is a good time to clean? I've a few hours before it's time to cook supper."

"Now is good. I'm heading to the mechanic. Figure I'll be gone at least an hour." Despite what she said, she did not look fine. She looked very upset. Liam sighed and grabbed the keys to his truck. If she didn't want to tell him what was wrong, then it was none of his business.

When she started wiping the counters, he marched to his truck.

Having her in his house, cleaning and cooking, was a whole lot different than his previous cook, Mrs. Jensen—plump and middle-aged—who had talked a mile a minute. Very different from the pretty, quiet Alisa. He thought he'd enjoy her silence, but the haunted look in her eyes a few minutes ago tugged at him. Something bothered his tenant. Something bothered her very much, and it had better not be one of his ranch hands. There'd be hell to pay. He turned around and stomped back into the house. "One of my men bothering you?"

"What?" She frowned up at him.

"Because if they are—"

"No. They are all perfectly respectful toward me."

"Good. I won't tolerate anything else." He stormed back out of the house and into his truck. Several seconds later, he sped to town, the truck brakes squealing every time he touched them, announcing his arrival at the mechanic.

"Hey, O'Ryan." Bill, the owner, wiped his hands on a dirty rag and strolled toward Liam's truck. "No need to tell me what needs fixin'. Heard you a mile away."

Liam climbed from the truck. "She's reliable for working around the ranch. Good thing I have my other vehicle. How long until she's ready?"

"Few days. I've just hired a new mechanic, but we're backed up." He jerked his head toward the garage. "Says he used to work for you. Name is Freddy Jones."

"Yeah, he did. I fired him for stealing." The man vowed he'd get even. Had he returned to town to make good on his promise?

Bill shrugged. "I'll watch him. He seems to know

his way around a vehicle."

Liam glanced over to see Freddy watching them with a stony expression on his face, a cigarette dangling from his lips. The man scowled, ground the cigarette under his foot, then went back into the garage when Liam met his stare.

"Bad blood, huh?"

"You could say that." Liam handed him the truck keys as Willy pulled into the lot. "Give me a call." He loped to the other vehicle and climbed in. "Thanks."

"Not a problem, boss." Willy backed out and headed toward the ranch.

"How are the other hands doing?"

"Good." Willy nodded. "Lars is kind of green, but he'll get a grip on things."

"How are they around Miss Gosling?"

"Fine, why? Want me to keep a closer eye on them?"

"If you wouldn't mind. Something has her spooked."

Willy gave a quick jerk of a nod. "She's gone most of the day, and the guys stay pretty busy, but I'll let you know if I see anything."

"Appreciate it." He smelled the roast the minute he exited the truck and smiled. Alisa was a good cook, no doubt about it. He'd made the right decision in offering her free rent in exchange for food and cleaning. "See you at supper."

Liam headed for his office and the monthly reports. Tomorrow was payday for his men, and he wanted to make sure the numbers fell into place. This job fell on his shoulders after firing Freddy, who had been his accountant.

By the time Alisa rang the bell announcing supper, he had a headache. The ranch was barely running in the black. He'd have to figure out a way to bring more income in. Liam leaned back in his chair. There was room to board more horses, and he could sell a couple of cattle, but he'd really wanted to increase his herd not lessen it.

He joined the others at the large kitchen table where a roast, potatoes, carrots, and gravy filled the space. "Smells good."

Alisa smiled. "Hope it tastes as good as it smells."

"It will. You cooked it." He chuckled as pink tinted her cheeks.

The other men echoed his sentiments and started filling their plates. While they ate, Liam kept a close eye on the younger two. While they joked and flirted, they didn't do anything Liam deemed inappropriate. In fact, they treated Alisa as they might a younger sister or the sister of a friend.

Or was Lars cutting her sly glances? He couldn't be positive. It was also likely he looked for something sinister where it didn't exist. Liam ducked his head and ate. When he'd finished, he helped Alisa clear the table.

"You don't have to. It's my job." She stood by the kitchen sink filling with hot water and soapy bubbles.

"I don't mind. It helps me clear my head." Which was true. "I'll wash and you dry."

"I'm not dumb enough to turn down help. Thank you." She blinked up at him like an adorable brown-eyed owl, then nodded.

They worked in silence, the water and scent of the bubbles doing a lot to calm Liam's worries until he caught Alisa casting her third worried look toward her rental. "Something is bothering you. Want to talk about it?"

She shook her head. "I'm fine."

"Are you expecting someone to be waiting for you when you go home?"

"Don't be silly." She set a stack of plates in the cupboard.

"Am I?" He pulled the plug from the drain. "Have it your way, but I'll be walking you home and checking the place out." Something had her spooked, and he'd be danged if he'd send her home alone. Staying close by her side, Liam escorted her to the little house out back. "Wait in the front room." It didn't take but a few minutes to declare the place empty. He checked to make sure all the windows and the back door were locked. "Everything looks fine. Do you want to sleep in the guest room in the main house tonight?"

"No, thank you. I'm being silly. Bad dreams last night."

He'd bet his favorite pair of boots she just lied to him. "Okay, but the offer is open if you need it. I'll leave the back door unlocked. Make sure this door is secure when I'm gone." He stepped out the front door, his gaze searching her face.

Some of the tension had left, smoothing out her features. Pressing his lips together, he nodded and marched toward the big empty house he called home.

Chapter Four

He gripped the phone tight enough to make his knuckles ache. "I don't care whether you think she knows anything or not. Follow her and make sure." What he wouldn't do for an old-fashioned phone he could slam the receiver down on. Instead, he pressed the off button with force and dropped the phone onto his desk.

Miss Gosling had fled Westport right after the secretary's murder. What if the secretary hadn't been the one to stumble across that letter? She hadn't shredded the forms as told to, so he'd assumed that when he hadn't found it in the garbage the cleaning woman had taken it. He had to be sure. That's why he needed to have her followed.

He wasn't against ordering someone's death, but he did draw the line at killing willy-nilly. His office chair creaked as he leaned back, propping his feet on his desk. One stupid employee's mistake could bring down his entire empire. That could not happen.

~

"Miss Gosling?"

Alisa turned to see Mr. Kingsley in the doorway of the bank. "Sir?"

"I'm hoping you have room in your schedule for

another client." He smiled. "Seems I'm minus a housekeeper at the moment."

"I'm sure I can squeeze you in." The man no doubt had a large house that would bring in much needed funds to her bank account. "I'll stop by this afternoon, if that's all right."

"Any time after five, thank you." Mr. Kingsley handed her a business card. "Address is on the back." He gave her a nod and stepped back inside the building.

She tucked the card in the pocket of her jeans. Things were going quite well for her in Misty Hollow despite the occasional bout of paranoia. If she'd been followed, if Mr. Barker thought she knew something, he'd have sent someone after her by now. It had been almost a month with no trouble.

The odor of cigarette smoke tickled her nostrils. She wrinkled her nostrils and turned to see a man in coveralls step from around the corner.

"Excuse me, ma'am." He stepped around her and crossed the street.

She coughed and entered the bookstore. Since it didn't open for another thirty minutes, she had time to clean the restrooms.

"Good morning, Alisa." Carol, the owner, smiled from behind her desk. "Nice day, isn't it?"

"Gorgeous." She carried her supplies into the men's room. Someday, she'd come to the bookstore to browse and enjoy a blended mocha coffee. Between her clients and the ranch, she had little time for simply relaxing. That needed to change. Why hadn't she asked Liam for days off? She vowed to do so as soon as she returned. She might be receiving free rent, but she deserved time off. At least one day a week to do things she wanted to.

When she finished with the men's room, she cleaned the women's. With a glance at her watch, she realized she did have a few minutes to herself. "I know the store isn't open yet, but I'll have to run soon." She stopped in front of Carol. "Do you mind if I browse a bit? I'd like a good book to wind down with in the evening."

"What genre?"

"Mystery and thriller." She grinned.

"There's a table of new releases at the front of the store. Pick what you want, and I'll give you twenty-five percent off."

"Thank you!" She set her supplies near the back door and rushed to the front of the store.

Her steps faltered as she saw the smoking man looking in the window. Spotting her, he nodded and continued on his way. No doubt, he was only window-shopping on his way to work. Alisa shook off the notion that his gaze had been fixed on her and not the table of books.

She chose two novels by different authors and returned to Carol to pay for her purchase. "I'm getting out just in time," she said, noting the clock said two minutes before nine o'clock.

Carol laughed. "You aren't a leper. Surely, the customers realize my bathrooms need cleaning."

"True. See you in the morning." She retrieved her supplies and headed to her car down the street. Businesses done, she now had a couple of houses to clean. She turned the key in the ignition and pulled away from the curb.

The smoking man was standing in the parking lot of Bill's Garage. He nodded and stomped out his cigarette as she passed.

Some of the tension left her shoulders and she gave a nervous laugh. The man had simply been walking to work, and they'd crossed paths. Nothing more.

Alisa texted Liam that she'd be late because she had to visit a new client. She should've thought of that when Mr. Kingsley said after five o'clock. The ranch hands worked hard and needed their meals on schedule.

Parking in front of a sprawling red-brick house that looked far too rich for the town of Misty Hollow, she cut the engine. The sweeping lawn was clear of trees. Landscaping was kept to a minimum, leaving all the focus on the house. Pretentious to say the least. She'd take a quick tour, see what the man wanted done, then give him a quote.

The banker met her on the front porch. "Welcome." He peered around her. "No supplies?"

"I'm sorry, but I'll have to return tomorrow to clean. If you accept my quote, that is." She arched a brow. "I also cook for the Leaning O Ranch, and I'm already late." Her mind raced to think of something quick she could fix when she returned.

"Not a problem."

He gave her a quick tour, handing her a long list of things to do each week. She quoted him a hundred dollars an hour and two days a week. The man didn't blink an eye.

Alisa smiled on her way back to her car. She wouldn't need to find anymore clients.

~

Liam had a big pot of spaghetti on the stove when Alisa arrived home and was slathering garlic spread on bread. Buddy, hoping he'd drop something, sat next to him, his dark eyes fixed on every move Liam made.

"I'm so sorry." She rushed into the kitchen. "Mr. Kingsley at the bank hired me to clean his house, and I couldn't take the tour until after five."

"It's not a problem." He smiled. "I enjoy cooking sometimes."

"Thank you." She started to say something else, then turned to stir the pot instead.

"Do you want to tell me something?"

"I want Sundays off. No cleaning, no cooking, nothing."

What a fool he'd been. He'd taken her for granted. "Yes. I'm sorry for not offering it before. I work every day and just…well…"

"I want to explore the town, the woods, that beautiful mountain. I want to see the mist hover over the valley in the morning. I want to read. I'd like to borrow a horse and ride once in a while."

"Read?"

"Yes. A book. Surely, you've heard of them."

He laughed. "Of course, I have. My mother has…there's a library here. You must have seen it. Feel free to borrow anything you'd like. As for the horse, all you have to do is ask whichever of us men are around to get one for you."

"Really?" Her eyes widened with pleasure.

"Yes. And, if you can stand my company, I'd like to show you that mist on Sunday. We'll head up the mountain before the sun rises." Why in the world was he offering to spend her only day off with her? Couldn't he take a hint? She'd pretty much stated she wanted time to herself.

"That sounds wonderful."

"It does?" He dropped the knife in his hand.

"You must think so or you wouldn't have invited me." She smiled. "I did say I wanted to see the mist, didn't I? Who better to show me than someone who's lived here a while?"

Until the arrival of Alisa first thing that one morning, he hadn't realized how lonely he'd been. The ranch hands were employees—even Willy who had been there for twenty years. Alisa had the right idea. A person couldn't work twenty-four seven. Liam stayed too busy for friends or a relationship.

He cut a sideways glance at the woman by the stove. No, he'd be her friend, nothing more. His life didn't leave much room for anything more. "I'll go ring the bell," he said, as she drained the spaghetti and turned off the flame under the sauce.

As he reached for the old-fashioned iron bell hanging from the porch, he spotted Lars on the opposite side of the corral talking to Freddy Jones. His eyes narrowed as the man tossed a still burning cigarette on the ground.

Without rain for a few weeks, the place was a tinderbox. Liam rang the bell harder than necessary, taking a bit of pleasure in seeing how the two men jumped. Jones shouldn't even be here. When Liam had fired him, he'd told the man never to step foot on his property again. He'd have to speak with Lars about him.

He watched as Jones slipped into the woods and Lars headed for the house. When he reached the back porch, Liam said, "That man isn't allowed on my property."

"I wasn't aware of that. We're friends, and I invited him over to see the new foal. It won't happen again." He brushed past Liam, his shoulder bumping his. Accident or a sign of aggression?

"How often is Jones here?" He asked Willy when he arrived.

"First time I've seen him. I'd have run him off otherwise. You know that, boss."

"I do, and I appreciate it. I'm taking Sunday off to show Alisa around. Can you cover for me?"

"Sure, I can." He grinned. "As long as I can take Saturday."

Liam felt even worse knowing he allowed his men to take off one day a week and hadn't offered Alisa the same. No, she had to tell him. "It's a deal."

After the meal, Liam washed while Alisa dried, something that had become routine for them. He listened while she told him about the two books she'd purchased from the bookstore.

"I can't wait to get to my house and start reading. It's better than watching TV."

"You think so? Give me an action film any day."

"No, a good thriller where people die and then justice is served is way better."

"I would've thought you'd be a romance kind of gal."

She shuddered. "Perfect people, perfect lives, and too stupid to see what they have until it's almost gone? No thank you."

"Come on. I'll walk you home so you can start your bloodthirsty evening." He drained the water out of the sink.

She laughed and headed for the door, then stopped, her laugh cutting off.

Liam stepped in front of her as Buddy growled.

Across the lawn, the end of a cigarette glowed red in the darkening evening. Jones again.

"You know him?"

She shook her head. "I saw him around town a few times today, but that's it. Do you?"

"Yes. He used to work for me. Stay here." Liam marched down the porch steps toward Jones.

Jones tossed his cigarette down and darted away.

Liam put out the cigarette. He'd have to contact Sheriff Westbrook tomorrow and put out a restraining order on the man.

"Is he dangerous?" Alisa stepped to his side.

"I doubt it, but he wasn't happy when I fired him." He put a hand on the small of her back, enjoying the warmth of her skin through the tee-shirt. "I doubt he'll be back tonight. Enjoy your book and lock your doors." He wanted to ask her to stay in the main house, but she'd say no. Alisa Gosling valued her independence.

"Good night, Liam." She entered her house and closed the door.

He didn't move until her heard the lock engage.

Chapter Five

Alisa slipped into comfortable shoes and grabbed her cell phone. She wanted to capture the magic of the mist hovering over the valley. And, if she were honest with herself, she looked forward to a fun day with Liam. Something not employer and employee or landlord and tenant.

She joined him in the kitchen, pleased to see him packing a backpack with sandwiches, a thermos, and bottles of water. "This must be going to take a while."

"Breakfast sandwiches." He grinned. "It's a short hike once we park. We'll have to hoof it to make it in time."

"Then let's go." She headed out the front door to his truck and climbed into the passenger seat. Buddy jumped in and sat between her and Liam, staring straight ahead through the front windshield like some four-legged chaperone.

Liam rubbed the dog's head, then turned the key in the ignition. "He's always up for a hike."

It seemed silly to be so excited about a day off on the mountain which showed Alisa just how much she needed the break. "I may be more excited than the dog." She hooked her seatbelt around her and settled in to enjoy the scenery.

They passed fields of tall grass meant to be hay, wildflowers, and trees with spring blossoms' beauty. Not that she could see all the colors in the predawn, but she could imagine. The mountain must be gorgeous in the fall. Hopefully, she'd be around to see it.

Liam parked the truck on the side of the road about halfway up Misty Mountain. "We walk from here. About a mile. Not too bad."

Since Alisa stayed busy every day, the mile wouldn't be bad at all. Cleaning houses was physical work that kept her in shape. She followed Liam's broad back through the trees until they reached a rock that jutted out over…nothing. Whoa. She stepped back, overcome by vertigo.

Liam grabbed her arm. "Afraid of heights?"

"I didn't think so, but I…we're very high up." She sat a safe distance from the edge. "I'll see just fine from here."

He sat next to her, his shoulder brushing hers, and dug the sandwiches from the backpack. "Egg and bacon."

Her stomach growled in response. "Coffee?"

"Right here." He handed her a thermos. "Hope you don't mind sharing."

"Share my coffee? Heaven forbid." She laughed and removed the lid, not minding in the slightest.

"There."

The sun lit the sky just enough to allow her to see the fog hovering over the valley below. Alisa gasped at the magical view. "It looks as if a person could walk on the clouds," she whispered, not wanting to ruin the magic by disturbing the silence. Not even birds twittered from the trees. She snapped a photo with her phone.

"Keep watching." Liam spoke close to her ear, his breath tickling the small hairs there.

The sun rose further, painting the sky rose and pumpkin. The colors reflected on the top of the mist. Alisa felt as if she were in a rainbow. Tears sprang to her eyes. She took another photo.

Alisa had never seen anything so beautiful and knew she'd found her favorite spot on earth. She wrapped her arms around her knees and watched until the sun burned away the mist revealing the town below. "I never want to leave here."

Liam chuckled. "It's my favorite start to a day. I try to make it up here a couple of times a month, even in the winter."

"I'd like to have a house up here and wake up to that every morning." But, she had things to do on her day off and couldn't stay on the mountain all day no matter how tempting. She needed to shop for a few groceries for her place, the list Liam had given her for the house, and she wanted to read on the back deck with nothing to look at but the pasture and woods.

Alisa scrambled to her feet and took one last look at the town below. Yes, she'd found the place where she belonged. Her home. Nothing would drive her away. She peered up into Liam's face. "Thank you."

His lips curled into a soft smile. "Thank you for loving it as much as I do." He slung the backpack over one shoulder, then took her hand in his free one. "Come on, Buddy."

They strolled back to the truck in companionable silence. Strange how his holding her hand made the day that much more special.

Alisa paused to enjoy the singing of the waking birds. "Oh." She stopped and motioned to where a doe and a spotted fawn stepped onto the path a few feet in front of them.

The fawn dashed into the foliage, while the mother pranced and danced, keeping their attention on her while the baby got away.

Buddy woofed, sending her bounding after her baby.

The day started as perfect as possible. She'd never seen a deer dance that way before. Alisa smiled and continued toward Liam's vehicle. This was only the first of as many mornings as possible.

~

"He ran me off. Not much I can do about that."

He wanted to smash the phone against the top of his desk. "Find another way to keep an eye on her. O'Ryan's ranch is big enough, so there ought to be plenty of hiding places. Get your friend to help you. If all else fails, make life miserable for them. As a last resort, we'll dispose of the woman. Leave some subtle hints. Use that brain in your thick skull."

"He doesn't want to get involved." The man's voice hardened. "I'm not some lackey you can boss around. You came to me, remember?"

"You'll do what I tell you. Make it worth your friend's time." He punched the off button. Why was good help so hard to find? He was paying the man a lot of money to keep an eye on Miss Gosling. Maybe some threats would make him more cooperative.

Drumming his fingers on his desk, he had to know whether she knew anything, suspected anything, or made copies of the letter. There had to be a way to get in that little house she lived in and snoop around. That's why he needed the ranch hand's help. No one would suspect him nosing around.

He'd think of something. Pasting on a smile, he went to unlock the doors at precisely nine o'clock. Business stopped for no one.

~

Liam dropped Alisa off at her car, then headed straight for the sheriff's office. The reception area was full, all three seats taken. Not a large department by any means, but the sheriff usually got the job done.

Liam approached the receptionist and asked to speak with the sheriff and was told it would be a few minutes because they were swamped. He agreed to wait and moved away from the other folks waiting. Scantily dressed women in handcuffs. Prostitutes? That would be a first for Misty Hollow.

"Mr. O'Ryan? The sheriff will see you now." The receptionist waved him down the hall.

"Thank you." Ignoring the scowls from those still waiting, he entered the sheriff's office. "Thank you for seeing me."

"Have a seat, Liam. It's good to see a friendly face. We're busier around here than a one-armed paper hanger. Seems like Misty Hollow has finally been infiltrated with prostitution and drugs."

Liam frowned. "You think we have organized crime here?"

"It's something I'm looking into. What can I do for you?" He folded his hands on the top of his desk and fixed his gaze on Liam.

"I'd like you to talk with Freddy Jones about staying away from my ranch."

"Why not get a restraining order?"

"I thought about it, but you and I both know they don't do a lot of good. I've seen him hanging around. I think he's watching my cleaning lady for some reason. Call it instinct." Liam had learned a long time ago to listen to his gut.

"I can send a deputy to speak with him but can't guarantee it'll be today." He jotted a note on his desk blotter.

"That works for me. Thanks." Liam stood. "Good luck with the new rash of crime."

"Let me know if you see or hear anything. You've been around long enough to know when something isn't right." Sheriff Westbrook turned to his computer.

Dismissed, Liam headed out of the building. Spotting Alisa driving past, he followed her, guessing she was headed to the grocery store. His guess was correct. He parked next to her.

"Need help?" He grinned.

"Your list is quite long." She returned his smile. "I'll finish faster if we divvy things up, but don't you have work to do?"

"Took the day off, remember? Willy can handle the ranch."

Alisa tore the list in half. "Meet you at the register." She grabbed a shopping cart and rushed away.

He glanced at the piece of paper in his hand. Wonderful. She'd given him the meat and produce. His favorite part. He'd have cringed with dry foods. No particular reason other than he didn't like processed anything.

Forty-five minutes later, cart full, he waited near the registers for Alisa. His jaw clenched when he caught sight of Jones in the self-serve lane. He wanted to confront the man but held back. It wouldn't help his case any if he did try to order a restraining order but made any move that could be construed as aggressive. So, they shared glares like a couple of hormonal teenagers until Alisa pushed her cart next to his.

"This thing is heavy. I've separated my personal items from the ranch's."

"Load yours on the belt first." He watched as Jones sauntered from the store, snaking his arm around the waist of a woman Liam didn't know. A woman dressed an awful lot like the ones in the sheriff's office.

"What's wrong?" Alisa started adding her things to the belt.

"Nothing." He erased the frown from his face. No reason to ruin her day with worries of his own.

After loading the majority of the groceries into his truck, he followed Alisa back to the ranch, taking note of folks he passed. He didn't see any more women like the ones in the sheriff's office or any strangers hanging around on street corners. Hopefully, things had been taken care of before crime could get a good grip on Misty Hollow. The town had already had its fair share of trouble in the last year or so.

At least this time no one had been murdered.

Liam took the ranch groceries into the main house while Alisa took her own home. It was her day off after all. Guess he'd be cooking again. He eyed the steaks he'd purchased and smiled. Grilled T-bones were on the menu for that night with baked potatoes.

As he grabbed the last of the bags, he noticed Lars leaning against the corral, his gaze fixed on Alisa's house. Liam surveyed the area to make sure there wasn't anything else the man could be looking at. There wasn't. He coughed loud enough to attract the hired man's attention, then jerked his head toward the barn. Liam wasn't paying the man to stare at his tenant.

Something was up not only in Misty Hollow but on the Leaning O Ranch. Liam intended to find out what.

Chapter Six

Already tired from cleaning the bank manager's house, Alisa carried her cleaning supplies into Liam's house and set them on the kitchen counter. Through the window, she spared a few seconds to watch him put a horse through its laps. She'd never tire of watching him, shirtless in tight jeans, working with a beautiful horse.

Darn it. She'd left her floor cleaner in the trunk of her car. That's what exhaustion did to a person. Alisa tossed Liam a wave as she retrieved the forgotten item from her trunk, then remembered the new can of furniture polish still in the bag on her counter. With a mental palm to the forehead, she retrieved the item from her kitchen, then hurried back to the main house. If she didn't hurry, supper would be late which filled her with guilt since the men worked hard all day, too.

She cleaned the kitchen like a whirling dervish, getting her second wind. Then, standing in the doorway that led to the dining room, she couldn't help but feel a sense of accomplishment. Sure, the room would need straightening again after supper, but once a month she gave the house more than just a straightening and today was the only time she had free on her schedule.

The floor above her head creaked. As far as she knew, she was the only one in the house. Chalking it up to the house settling, she grabbed a dustrag and dusting spray and entered the living room.

The creak sounded again. "Liam?" Maybe he entered through the front door while she'd been cleaning the kitchen.

With no response, she returned to the kitchen. No sign of Liam in the corral. Alisa shrugged and returned to work. Not much later, she lugged the supplies upstairs. She turned the knob on the door to the main bathroom and pushed it open.

Her nose burned, her eyes watered. Her breath wheezed. Slamming the door shut, she felt her way to the top of the stairs, taking big gulps of air tainted with toxic fumes. Alisa made it almost all the way to the bottom before falling, thankfully only tumbling down the last three steps.

She fell on her elbow, knocking the breath from her, and lay on the floor she'd just cleaned like a stranded fish. Tears ran down the sides of her face, soaking her hair. Was that movement at the top of the stairs? She couldn't be sure.

"Alisa?" Liam stepped from the kitchen and leaned over her, Buddy at his side. "Are you all right? Hurt?"

"Bathroom." She forced the word from her tortured throat.

His brow furrowed, and he thundered up the stairs.

"No!" Her word sounded more like a squeal than a shout. "Cover your mouth and nose." She forced herself into a sitting position, thankful she could breathe well enough to give him a warning.

Minutes later, his eyes red, he joined her on the

bottom step. He lowered the neckline of his tee shirt from his nose and mouth. "You mixed ammonia and bleach?"

"Of course not." She scowled. "I know better than that. Heard someone upstairs while I was cleaning."

"Are you sure?" He glanced at the ceiling above them. "There's no other way down." He stood. "Stay here. I'll check it out. Or…" he peered closer at her face. "Do you need medical attention?"

She shook her head. "I'd only opened the door. I'll be fine in a few minutes."

With a nod, he climbed the stairs, slower this time.

Alisa moved to the kitchen and rinsed her face and eyes with water. Within a few minutes, the burning had eased, and she drank big gulps of water from the bottle on the counter. When she turned, a stony-faced Liam stood in the doorway.

"Someone climbed out a guest window. I found the nylon rope they used. It's still tied to the bed."

Alisa sagged against the corner. They found her.

Liam rushed forward and lowered her into a chair. "I think you need to go to the ER."

"No, it isn't that." How could she tell him she had brought trouble to the ranch? He'd fire her on the spot.

"Why would someone come into my house and mix dangerous chemicals together, Alisa?" He crossed his arms. "What are you not telling me?"

She told him about finding the ripped-up paper at Barker Construction, the murdered receptionist, then about her fleeing to Misty Hollow. "I thought if I left, pretended I hadn't seen anything, I'd be left alone."

"A woman was killed?" His expression switched from anger to concern in the blink of an eye. "If they think you know something—"

"I've brought trouble here."

He exhaled heavily. "Did you make a copy?"

"Yes," she whispered. "I mean, I took a photo of it with my phone. I turned over the main pieces to the Westport police."

"I need to call the sheriff. Find the photo on your phone and send it to my email, then delete it. We'll hand it over and be done."

It wasn't going to be that easy.

~

He'd watched her stumble back from the bathroom and down the stairs. Watched from the top as she'd fallen and lay there. Had she seen him through the tears in her eyes?

His plan couldn't have worked more perfectly. The boss would be pleased at the warning he'd left. That's why he hadn't taken the rope with him. He wanted O'Ryan and the pretty cleaning lady to know someone had been inside. Someone who could do them harm.

Since she'd turned over the letter to the police, it didn't take a genius to know she'd known something was going on with Barker Construction. She wasn't an idiot. The girl would be telling O'Ryan all she knew. He'd call the sheriff. An investigation might start.

The boss didn't want that to happen. Hopefully, Miss Gosling would keep her mouth shut.

If not, he'd have to shut it for her, and he didn't like harming women. But, he'd do what the boss ordered. When it came between living and principles, living won out every time.

~

Liam called the sheriff's office and was patched straight through to the sheriff's private phone. "We had a break-in. Someone tried to harm Miss Gosling."

"I can be there in fifteen minutes. Don't leave her alone." He hung up.

Liam took Alisa by her arm and led her to the living room. "Stay here. I'm going to lock up." He pulled the double French doors closed behind them, then secured the front and back doors before joining her in the living room.

"This isn't your fault," he told her. "Anyone could have found those papers. What I'd like to know is why they weren't shredded."

She shrugged. "Negligence. I should've left the paper on the floor. I was already working late."

"Then you wouldn't have done your job." Liam took her hands in his, sorry to feel them tremble. "The sheriff will get to the bottom of this. He's good at what he does."

She tilted her head. "Really?"

"He's former FBI." He left out the part about the recent serial killer the sheriff hadn't known was one of his own deputies. While Liam respected the man, that case didn't fill him with a lot of optimism.

When a knock sounded on the door, he told Alisa to stay put, leaving Buddy to protect her, and went to lead the sheriff to the window the intruder had escaped out of. "He also mixed bleach and ammonia together, knowing Alisa would enter the bathroom to clean it."

"And there's a letter?"

"Yes. We'll print it off for you before you go." Spotting Willy, Liam pointed the sheriff in the right direction and went to tell his top hired man that supper would be late.

"Someone broke in?"

Liam nodded. "Was Dan and Lars around the last hour?"

"Yes. We had some horses to shoe. All three of us were in the barn all afternoon. Want me to order some pizzas? The guys won't care what they eat as long as their fed." He peered around Liam. "Out the window, you say? Would have to be someone light, not too heavy."

All four of the men on the ranch, including Liam, were fit. Hard work kept them trim and physically adept. "Pizza sounds great. Have it delivered to the outside picnic table. Alisa and I will join you when we're finished."

The sheriff stared at a footprint below the window. "Looks like a work boot, size elevenish."

"That could be any one of my men."

"Any of them have reason to want to harm Miss Gosling?"

"Not that I know of. Olson and James have been with me for a while. Avery is the newest. He's only worked for me for about three months. Longer than Miss Gosling has. I don't think it's one of my men, Sheriff." Liam compared the print to his foot. Size eleven exact.

The living room window opened. Alisa poked her head out. "I think you need to see the news." She withdrew, closing the window.

Liam glanced at the sheriff, then they both hurried into the house.

On the television, a news reporter stood in front of a burning office building.

"That's Barker Construction," Alisa said. "They suspect arson."

Liam shot another look at the sheriff. "What do we

do?"

"You do nothing but send me a copy of that letter. We'll handle things from here." He sighed. "One more thing on the to-do list."

"Any luck on the drugs and prostitution?"

"Nope. We lock up one and two more show up. It's almost as if someone wants me and my deputies too busy to see what's really going on in Misty Hollow."

While the sheriff went to investigate the room the intruder had escaped from, Liam went to his office and printed off the photo Alisa sent to his email. He read the letter. So, a threat to expose someone. Definitely not a letter someone with a secret would want to get out.

He deleted the email and took the letter upstairs to the sheriff.

"I'll get someone over here to case the scene. If possible, don't let anyone in the bathroom or this bedroom. No one else upstairs at all if you can help it. We've already contaminated evidence enough." Sheriff Westbrook turned from the window. "At least no one has died," he mumbled.

Yet. Liam followed him downstairs.

The sheriff froze at the sound of an arriving vehicle. "You expecting anyone?"

"Pizza delivery." Liam peered out the peephole. "Yep." He opened the door and stepped out.

"Let me know if you see anyone else suspicious hanging around." Sheriff Westbrook marched to his car.

"I'm sorry about supper. Again." Alisa stepped to his side. "I don't...well, I've..." She sighed so heavy Liam could feel her despair.

He gripped her shoulders and turned her to face him. "I'm only going to say this once more, and you are going to believe me. This is not your fault."

"I came here." Her chin quivered. "I didn't think lightening could strike twice. The same thing is going on here."

"You don't know that. This could have nothing to do with you and everything to do with the new rash of crime in town." He smiled. "Besides, I'm glad you came. You've been a big help to me with the cooking and cleaning. My men like and respect you. Heck, even Buddy likes you."

She bit off a laugh. "That is something."

"Come on. Let's join the others for that pizza and let the sheriff take over." He couldn't help but shoot a wary glance over his shoulder as they rounded the corner. No matter what he said about this being related to the recent crime, it surely centered around Alisa.

Chapter Seven

Mrs. Mayfield had tea and cookies ready when Alisa arrived to clean. "I do look forward to our weekly visit."

Gossip session more likely. Alisa was able to gather information on the residents of Misty Hollow without actually meeting them. But, she did like the older woman. "So do I."

"Did you see the news last night?" She handed Alisa a plate with two chocolate chip cookies.

"The fire in Westport?"

"No, the drug bust in Misty Hollow. It aired at ten p.m."

"I was asleep by then."

"At your age?" She tsked. "You need to go out more."

After someone tried to poison her with toxic fumes, Alisa had been more than happy to crawl into her bed and forget all about the hours prior to going to sleep. "I had a long day."

"You do too much, cooking and cleaning at the ranch, then cleaning other folks' houses. Why don't you find a real job, sweetie?" She poured tea into a cup. "I think they're hiring at the coffee shop.

"I have a real job." She frowned. "It's good money, and I'm my own boss."

"A man is what you need." She sat across from Alisa. "What do you think about the drugs and prostitution plaguing our fine town?"

"Haven't really noticed. Coming from the big city, it isn't much different." Which was an outright lie. She didn't want the troubles of the city to spoil this town.

"I guess you might be secluded out there on the ranch." Mrs. Mayfield added a heaping teaspoon of sugar to her tea. "Something is happening in this town, Alisa. Something dark and evil. One of our citizens is not what they appear."

Alisa shuddered, knowing it was her fault some of this was happening. Maybe not the drugs and prostitution but the trouble at the ranch. How long would it take before the town's residents learned she'd brought trouble to Liam?

"Heard you had a visitor at the ranch."

Not long obviously. "Word spreads fast."

"In this town? Like lightening." The old woman smiled, her face wrinkling. "Besides, Dane James is my grandson. You know, he works on the ranch. If I don't learn something myself, he always fills me in."

Alisa didn't think Liam would be pleased to hear one of his hands told Mrs. Mayfield about the ranch happenings. Even Alisa knew the woman, dear as she was, couldn't keep a secret. "An interrupted burglary attempt, we think. No one was harmed, and the sheriff is aware. Is there anyone new to town besides me?"

"No. That no-good Freddy Jones has returned, but he grew up here. Why do you ask?"

She shrugged. "Just wondering how many people

find out about Misty Hollow."

"The way the mountain shades us, not many stumble across us by accident. Most find us on the map from what I've heard. Isn't that how you found us?"

She nodded. "I wanted somewhere far away and completely different." She finished her cookies, took a big gulp of her tea, and pushed to her feet. "I'd best start working. Thank you for the tea and cookies."

"Be careful, sweetie. It's the newcomers who seem to suffer the most."

Her words of warning hung over Alisa as she cleaned. What did she mean? Did Misty Hollow not want newcomers? Was it that simple? Had Alisa simply picked the wrong place to relocate?

That didn't make any sense. She leaned on her mop. When she returned to the ranch, she'd ask Liam. He'd know what Mrs. Mayfield meant.

Since she only had the one house to clean, Alisa visited the bookstore for another couple of books. She could go to the library but preferred owning the books if she enjoyed them. A good book deserved to be read more than once.

"Good morning," the woman behind the desk greeted her. "More suspense and thrillers?"

"Absolutely." Alisa grinned.

"All you have to do is watch the news. Visit the diner. The drug bust is the big topic of conversation. Lately, we have all the suspense a person needs."

So, Alisa hadn't brought the trouble. Then why the intrusion at the ranch? Why the mix of chemicals? Or…. She'd brought her trouble to a place already being attacked by crime. The idea helped her feel a tiny bit better knowing it wasn't all her fault.

Alisa purchased two more books and headed for the diner. If this was the place to find out the gossip, she could spare a few dollars to buy a sandwich. She took a seat in a booth by the window and studied the menu. A BLT sounded perfect.

The waitress, a woman in her thirties, approached the table. "Haven't seen you before. Welcome to Lucy's."

"Thanks. I'm new to town. I'll have the BLT, chips, and a diet soda." She glanced to the lunch counter where two elderly men talked loud enough for her to hear.

"Hard of hearing," the waitress said, "so everyone here listens in." The woman smiled and promised to return with her order.

"I'm telling you—how do you think he affords that big house?" One of the men said. "It ain't because of his salary, I'll tell you that."

"Leave it be, Walt. It ain't none of our business. Sticking your big ole nose where it doesn't belong will get you into trouble."

"As a concerned citizen, it ain't right to sit back and do nothing. I'm going to tell the sheriff my suspicions. Ain't but one person in this town drives a fancy car, owns a mansion, and acts like he's God Almighty, and that's the bank manager." He slapped money onto the counter and marched from the diner.

Alisa's eyes rounded. The man might be onto something. She was the only person in town who had access to the banker's house other than the man himself. If she heard any more comments about him being behind the crime spree in this town—her home now, she might just have to do some snooping.

~

Freddy leaned against a lamppost and watched Alisa through the window of the diner. Between working at the garage and keeping an eye on her, he didn't have much time to enjoy the delights of the flood of women brought to town. It didn't make him happy, either. A man deserved some fun, didn't he?

The boss ought to understand since he brought the women here. Freddy paid the required amount for a bit of dope. He deserved it.

He pushed away from the lamppost as Alisa moved from the booth and paid her bill. When she exited the store, he ducked into the drugstore. She strolled down the sidewalk toward her car, not knowing he watched her. Not knowing he waited to hear from his boss as to how to handle her. If she didn't do anything stupid, nothing would happen to her.

Freddy wasn't sure if he wanted to have to rough her up. She hadn't done anything to him, but he did enjoy a woman who struggled. He stepped back outside and lit a cigarette before heading back to the garage.

~

Liam finished mucking out the stalls, then went to feed the cows. A newborn calf suckled at its mother. He smiled. "Good job, little lady. That's a fine little boy you have." One that would fetch a nice price at the auction.

He glanced toward the smaller corral where he had five head of cattle ready to sell. The sale would help his bottom line. Hopefully, the other pregnant cows would have girls. Not only did he want to have males to sell, but he needed females to increase his herd.

A truck pulling a horse trailer rumbled up the drive. Liam stopped what he was doing and went to greet them. "Can I help you?"

"Someone told me you board horses?" A man in overalls climbed from the truck.

"I do. Usually, folks call first to make sure I have room."

"Do you have room for two? My kids have gone to college, and I'm too busy for the horses."

Liam frowned. Animals weren't something to be played with for a while, then dumped on someone else to care for. "You could sell them?"

"Nah, the kids will ride them during their breaks."

Liam helped the man lead the two roans to the boarding barn. "We'll make sure they're cared for." He might not like them being cast off, but he did need the money. "Come see them any time. Someone is always here."

As the man drove away, Alisa was walking toward him with another bag from the bookstore. He shook his head. Why didn't she make use of his library?

"Can I ask you something?" She tilted her head, stopping in front of him.

"Of course."

"Mrs. Mayfield, one of my clients and the grandmother of one of your hands, knew about the break-in last night. She also told me Misty Hollow doesn't like newcomers. That something always happens to them. Is the last part true?"

"That's the silliest thing I've ever heard. The town isn't a living, breathing thing, Alisa. It can't target anyone."

"No, but the townspeople can." She hitched her chin. "Maybe they don't like outsiders."

"Has anyone been rude to you?"

"Well, no."

"Didn't you find clients your first week of being here?" He crossed his arms and arched a brow. "If they wanted you gone, you wouldn't have a single client."

"Okay. I'm just being silly." She then told him about a conversation between the two men at the diner.

He narrowed his eyes. "Don't go snooping."

"I won't unless it has something to do with me."

"Like what?"

She shrugged. "After last night, I'm not discounting anything." Alisa headed into her house.

Neither was he. The sheriff seemed as concerned as he'd been during the serial killer episode last fall. But, thinking the letter Alisa found at Barker Construction had anything to do with the local bank manager seemed like a stretch to Liam.

He entered the boarding barn and made sure the new additions were comfortable, then headed out the back door to the main barn. At the far end of the corral, Lars Avery stood in deep conversation with Freddy Jones. Enough was enough.

Liam strode toward them. "I've told you not to step foot on my property, Jones." He glared at the man then turned to Avery. "I won't tell you again."

"He just showed up, boss." Avery stepped back.

"Get to work." Liam kept his narrowed eyes on Jones. "What do you want?"

"Just visiting a friend."

"How do you know Avery?"

"Well, now, that isn't any of your business."

"It is when you won't stay away. I'll be alerting the sheriff." He glanced at the man's feet, noting the mud around the edges. "You didn't happen to pay us a visit last night, did you? Went into my house and tried to harm my employee? Because I'm thinking you did."

"My beef isn't with Miss Gosling." The man's lip curled.

"No, it's with me. Remember that. Now get off my property."

The man's eyes held a sharp glint of a promise Liam didn't want to see come to fruition. He'd be carrying a gun on his hip from now on.

Jones gave him a sarcastic salute and strolled past the house and down the road instead of through the woods as he usually did.

Liam turned to see Alisa watching from her doorway and joined her.

"I don't know who the target was last night," she said. "Seems you have problems of your own. Add in mine, and we have a situation."

He sure did.

Chapter Eight

He lay on the bed as Cherie, his favorite of the women, padded naked and barefoot to the master bathroom. He crossed his arms behind his head and smiled. Those under his control did everything he asked without question. One phone call, one word, and she'd arrived on his doorstep. He loved the feeling of power.

With Barker out of the way, and the fool who'd threatened him, things were definitely looking up. It hadn't been difficult to lure the author of the letter to Barker's office. The promise of money was always a good lure.

He rolled over to go to sleep. What was taking Cherie so long?

When he woke a short time later, she still hadn't returned to bed. He threw aside the sheet and headed to the master bathroom. The closet door hung open.

He stepped inside quietly. Cherie had somehow picked the closet safe and now sat with stacks of cash and papers around her.

"Curiosity killed the cat, Cherie.".

She gasped and whirled, eyes wide. "I, uh…"

Rage boiled within him, searing his blood. His fingers curled. "Who told you to snoop? What are you looking for?" Only an accomplished lock picker could have opened his safe. No one knew the combination but him. No one knew the safe was in his closet. It stayed concealed behind a wall of sock drawers. He leaned close. "Who do you work for?"

"You," she whispered.

"Who hired you to break into my safe? How did you find it?"

"I'm a thief. I know these things." She shrank back from him. "You're laundering money. You killed Barker. You're way into more than drugs and women." She squared her shoulders. "Make me a partner."

Smart woman. She thought if she could make him believe she wanted in, he wouldn't kill her. Unfortunately, he traveled light.

He landed a hard jab to her right jaw, knocking her on her back. Then, he straddled her and wrapped his fingers around her throat and squeezed. She bucked under him, her eyes turning red, then she slowly stilled as the life left her body.

~

Alisa sipped her coffee the next morning while listening to the news. A reporter stood in front of the burned-out Barker Construction office building. She pressed the volume button on the remote to increase the sound.

She slowly lowered to the sofa when the reporter mentioned arson and that the owner, Barker, and two of his workers had perished in the fire. Her hand trembled as she set her cup on the end table. Someone really wanted whatever evidence was left at Barker Construction to disappear, and arson was an excellent way to achieve it.

Several hours lay between Misty Hollow and Westport, but fear still trickled down her spine. There weren't enough miles between the two towns to make her feel safe.

Picking her cup back up, she left her little house and headed to Liam's to start flipping pancakes for breakfast. Anything to try and keep her mind off the newscast.

A fog hung over the property. The same mist engulfed the valley every morning. Usually, Alisa took her time walking to the main house but not today. The fog seemed to add a sinister touch to everything today.

She entered the kitchen to the sight of Liam sipping a cup of coffee. "What's wrong?" His brows lowered.

"They've determined the fire at Barker Construction was arson. Barker and two other men died in the blaze."

His gaze locked on hers for several tense minutes. "Westport is a ways from here. It's likely that has nothing to do with what we're dealing with."

"Maybe." She didn't believe in coincidences. She set her cup on the counter and went to the pantry to collect the ingredients for pancakes. "With the sudden increase in organized crime in Misty Hollow, and someone wanting to silence Barker…the letter was made out to him, though." She pulled a bowl from the cupboard. "Maybe the arsonist wrote the letter." Or maybe the person who wrote the letter was already dead.

"A lot of what ifs." He stood and set his cup in the sink. "I'll head to the shower. I think clearer there." He put a hand on her shoulder. "We'll be okay." After giving her a gentle squeeze, he left.

By the time he returned, she had the last of the pancakes in the pan and rang the bell to call in the hands. "Any insight from the shower?"

"No." He shrugged. "We'll keep our eyes and ears open. If what happened in Westport comes here, then we'll figure out what to do. No sense worrying about something that might not happen."

"We had a break-in."

"That had everything to do with me. Jones is holding a grudge, if it was him."

"Then why me?"

"Because you were an easy target."

Maybe, but Alisa wasn't convinced. Until she knew more, she'd go along with his assumption. But she wouldn't stand back and do nothing. Which meant asking questions. She'd have lunch at the diner as often as possible. Find out who the man was that suspected the bank manager and talk to him.

She ate quickly and started dishes before the men finished. "Busy day," she said in regard to Liam's raised brow. "I'm cleaning Mr. Kingsley's house today, and it takes a while."

She rushed through the cleaning of the bookstore restrooms and a couple of houses in town before heading to the diner a little before noon. The man she sought, Walt, climbed out of a beaten-up pickup truck. Alisa pulled up next to him and rolled down the window. "Sir, a minute, please?" Cutting the engine, she rushed from her car. "May I ask you a couple of questions?"

"You aren't trying to sell me anything, are you?" He crossed his arms and leaned against the front of his vehicle. "'Cause if I want something, I'll go to the store."

"I was in the diner yesterday and overheard you talking to your friend about Mr. Kingsley. Since I'm his housecleaner—"

"You couldn't pay me to step foot in his house. He's

a bad man, Miss."

"Why do you think that?"

"Look at his house, his car, the suits he wears. Very expensive for Misty Hollow. There aren't enough people in town to make the bank that big of a success." He lowered his voice. "Now there's the drugs, the loose women…it all makes sense. Someone brought them here, and my bet is on Kingsley."

"Do you have proof?"

He tapped his temple. "I have all the proof I need up here. It's called using my brain. You be careful over there, Miss. Keep your wits about you."

"I will, thank you." He'd given her nothing but his opinion.

Alisa followed him into the diner and ordered the day's special. She had time to loiter in case gossip circulated. After an hour with no new information, she headed to Kingsley's house.

Relief flooded through her when she didn't see his car out front. Alisa peeked in the garage window. No car there either. She could get in and out without having to see the man.

As usual, an envelope with her pay waited on the foyer table. She slipped it into her bag and lugged her cleaning supplies to the kitchen. With buds in her ears, she turned on her favorite sea shanty and started cleaning.

When it was time to take out all the garbage, she realized she'd run out of large bags. Surely, Kingsley had some. Most people did. She searched the pantry and came up empty. Nothing under the sink either.

Alisa headed for the garage and flicked on the overhead fluorescent lights. She found a roll of black lawn-and-leaf bags which would do the trick and noticed a bag in the corner. One of her jobs was to take out the garbage. Why would this bag be left out of the way where she might not notice? She undid the tie around the bag, opened it, and peered inside.

Over-processed hair tickled her hand. Alisa peered closer. The dead stare of a woman sent her careening.

With a scream she raced for the front door, taking her supplies with her. No, wait. She couldn't let there be any signs of having discovered the woman. Alisa returned the bags to where she'd found them and closed the bag containing the woman, averting her gaze from the dead eyes. She'd seen this woman before, alive and hanging on that mechanic's arm.

Had he killed her and left her here or had Kingsley committed the crime? Nausea rose, burning her throat as she backed away from the body in the bag. Then, she retrieved her cleaning supplies as quickly as possible, made sure everything looked just as she usually left it, and darted for her car.

~

"Liam!"

He dropped the pitchfork and raced for the barn door.

Alisa sprinted across the lawn, fear etched across her pale face.

"What happened?"

She rushed past him. "Close the door. Please."

He stepped in and pulled the double doors closed. "You're scaring me, Alisa. What's going on?"

"Are we alone?" She sent furtive glances around the barn. "The back door? The loft?"

"I'll check the loft. You check the back door." Her

fear was contagious. The hair on his arms stood at attention as he climbed the ladder to the hayloft, expecting a knock to the head as he cleared the top rung. The loft was empty.

"Clear." He put his hands on her shoulders. "Tell me."

"I found a dead woman in Kingsley's garage."

"Sit down." He lowered her to a three-legged milking stool. "Say that again?"

"I couldn't find trash bags, so I…oh, no. I didn't take out the garbage." Her eyes rounded. "I have to let him know I ran out of bags or he'll suspect something."

"Slow down. You're in no condition to call anyone, much less a man with a dead body in his garage. I did hear you right, didn't I?"

She nodded. "I was just looking for bags."

"Did you recognize the woman?"

"Yes. I saw her at the grocery store with that mechanic."

So, one of the prostitutes. He paced the barn floor. "We'll have to call the sheriff."

"No. I'm the only one in the house today. He'll know it was me who said something if the law shows up."

"If we don't, the body will disappear."

"Maybe Kingsley didn't kill her. Maybe he's being framed. I can't work for a killer, Liam." She covered her face with her hands.

He needed to think. If they didn't call the sheriff, they'd be breaking the law. They could go to jail. Surely, the sheriff could find a way to search the house and leave Alisa out of it.

"Call Kingsley. Tell him you finished but couldn't

take out the garbage because you ran out of bags. Tell him you'll be back tomorrow if that's okay. He won't suspect anything if you're willing to go back. Don't let him hear the fear in your voice."

She nodded and placed the call. "I left a message on his voicemail."

"Good. Now, we're going to pay a visit to the sheriff."

She shook her head hard enough to cause some hair to escape her ponytail.

"Yes. He'll know how to keep you out of this." Liam took her hand and pulled her to her feet. "We'll be okay. I promise."

"You can't promise that." She yanked her hand free. "Things are escalating. I found a dead body!"

"Shh." Liam clamped a hand over her mouth as something clattered just outside. He rushed to the window in time to see Jones fleeing into the trees.

Chapter Nine

No one would dare expect him. Kingsley studied himself in the men's room of the bank. Every hair in place, a fitted suit that cost more than most of these hicks made in a month, or a year. His hands were clean, no defensive wounds anywhere. Who would miss a prostitute other than the one who sent her? Draw that person out of the sewer and he'd find his nemesis.

His heart stopped when his phone rang earlier, and he'd seen Miss Gosling's number on the screen. But, then, he'd realized she wouldn't call him if she'd found Cherie. She'd have called the sheriff, who would have shown up by now. Nothing to worry about. He called Jones and ordered him to dispose of the body immediately.

"It's too late."

Kingsley frowned. "What do you mean?"

"I heard the cleaning lady say she found a dead body."

Then why hadn't the sheriff shown up at the bank? "You must have heard wrong. They're on a ranch. Could have been a dead cow for all you know. Find out what she knows and take the next step."

"What's that, boss?"

"Give her a message she can't miss." He hung up and returned to his desk. If Jones was correct about what he'd heard, then Kingsley needed to act as if nothing was wrong. Work as usual. He also needed a plan to lay the blame on someone else if the sheriff did ask questions.

He spotted Wilbur, the town's one and only homeless man who lived in a tent by the lake, and rushed outside to have a word. "Want to make a few bucks?"

"Sure. I'm always up for a job." The man smiled through his beard.

"I have a light not working properly in my master closet. The bulbs are in the garage. Replace it and check all the others." He pulled a hundred-dollar-bill from his wallet. "Have it done within the hour?"

"I'll head right on over there."

Perfect. While the man was dropping DNA like bird seed, Kingsley would do some planting of his own in the man's tent. A bit of meth, some porn magazines, and the stage would be set.

~

Sheriff Westbrook stood like one of the guards outside Buckingham Palace as Alisa recounted what she'd seen that morning. A muscle ticked in his jaw. He rarely blinked. When she finished, he glanced out the kitchen window toward the woods. "You sure he heard you?"

She nodded. "Liam saw him take off. I can't have Mr. Kingsley know I…" She shuddered.

"We'll keep that part quiet. I'll find another reason to question the man. O'Ryan, I'm strongly suggesting you take out that restraining order on Jones. It will give us legal ground if he returns."

"I'll do that this week. Today, I'm picking up my

truck." Liam glanced at Alisa. "I'll keep an eye on her, too."

"Keep to your usual schedule as much as possible, Miss Gosling. Do your best to act as if you didn't find a woman dead. Can you do that?" The sheriff turned his stony eyes back to her.

"Yes." If she couldn't, she might find herself stuffed in a bag. How would she be able to face Kingsley? Avoiding him, cleaning his house…Oh, Lord, could she continue as his cleaning lady? But she had to. She'd make sure he wasn't home when she cleaned. Alisa wrapped her arms around her waist to fight off a chill that came from inside. "I'll be fine."

Liam shot her a worried look before turning back to the sheriff. "We'll let you know if we hear or see anything else."

The sheriff nodded and strode to his car.

The three ranch hands hovered near the corral, clearly interested in why the sheriff had been on the ranch. "What will you tell them?" Alisa jerked her head in their direction.

"That I called him out about Jones not staying away. They don't need to know more than that. Let me take care of this. Would you rather I have one of them take me to pick up my truck?"

"No, I can take you. I need to pick something up from the store." Toothpaste and toiletries. Insignificant things after a woman had been killed.

"Okay. I'll meet you by your car in fifteen minutes. We need to return before it rains."

Alisa peered at the darkening sky as she went into her house and splashed cold water on her face. She stared at her reflection in the mirror. Why her? Why did she have to find that letter? Why couldn't they have disposed of the letter properly? She'd be none the wiser and not running for her life.

Misty Hollow hadn't been far enough away. Maybe there was nowhere in the state or even the country where she could hide.

Alisa gripped the edge of the pedestal sink. No! She wouldn't allow Kingsley and whoever worked for him to drive her away. This was her home now, and she'd stand and defend it to the best of her ability.

After the little pep talk, she squared her shoulders and marched to her car where Liam waited, his hand on Buddy's head. Since she'd hurtled from the driver's seat, her purse and keys were still inside. Thieves didn't worry her on the ranch.

"You don't mind if he comes along, do you? He likes riding in the truck." Liam crooked a smile.

"Not at all." She climbed in. "Do you know a man named Walt?"

"Sure. He's lived here all his life. Why?" He clicked his seatbelt into place.

She turned the key in the ignition. "He was in the diner telling another man that he thought Kingsley was behind the crime in town. I asked him to tell me more, but he was just mouthing off about Kingsley's house, his suits, and his car. But Walt is right. I want to find him and warn him without actually telling him about the dead woman. How do I do that?"

"I don't see how you can. I'll stop by the sheriff's office and tell him about Walt. Hopefully, a deputy can keep a watchful eye on the man and convince him to keep his theories to himself for a while."

~

Liam hooked Buddy's leash to a tree outside the sheriff's office and went to speak to the sheriff. "This won't take long," he said after being told to head back. "I don't even need to sit down. You know Walt Donaldson? He's been spouting off at the diner about how he thinks Kingsley is the man behind the surge in crime. Thought you might want to convince him to be quiet for a bit."

"Things get muddier and muddier around here." Westbrook pressed a button on his desk phone. "Send Deputy Miller in here." He removed his finger from the button. "Thanks, Liam. Have you ever considered law enforcement?" He grinned. "Lately, you've been right in the thick of things."

Liam laughed. "I have enough to do." Especially since finding Alisa gasping at the bottom of his stairs. Things had escalated from there.

He retrieved Buddy and headed down the sidewalk toward Bill's Garage. "Got a message my truck is ready."

Bill slid from under a raised sedan. "Sure is. Keys are in it."

"Who did the work?"

"I did. Since you and Jones don't exactly like each other, I thought it best."

"Where is he?"

"Didn't show up today. Jones worked late last night. I figure he hit the bar afterward. Sleeping it off. Just drop the money inside." He rolled back under the sedan.

Liam dropped the money on the man's cluttered desk. The whole room smelled like oil and gas. A bucket of rags sat in a corner. The place was a tinderbox waiting for a spark to start an inferno.

Shaking his head, he led Buddy to the truck. "Let's take this rattletrap home, boy." He waved at Alisa who strolled toward the drugstore. She waved back, then went inside.

"Maybe I'll cook tonight. What do you say?" Liam opened the door to the truck to let Buddy in. "Give Alisa a break. She works too hard. We don't want her quitting on us." Not to mention how he'd become used to seeing her every day. The ranch wouldn't be the same if she were to leave.

He couldn't believe how after a month's time, his gaze searched for her when he stepped outside. How he looked to see whether her light was off before going to sleep himself. "I think I might be feeling toward her in a way I don't want." The ranch took all his time and energy. Taking off that one Sunday had stretched him thin. How could he even think about a relationship? "Need to switch directions pronto, Buddy."

He steered the truck out of the lot and headed down to the valley where the ranch nestled just as the clouds overhead thickened and swirled. It would pour soon, most likely before he reached home.

Buddy whined out the open window.

"It'll be okay. We'll be home soon." He reached over and gave the dog a quick scratch behind the ears, then returned both hands to the steering wheel as the road steepened.

He pressed the brake to slow down. The pedal went to the floor.

Liam sucked in a sharp breath, then pumped the pedal. "So much for getting the brakes fixed," he muttered. "They're worse. Hold on, Buddy."

His knuckles ached from his tight grip. To his right,

the impenetrable mountain. To his left, a whole lot of treetops. It was going to be a mad ride.

Chest tight and a twitch near his right eye, Liam focused on not driving off the road. Buddy's whines increased as the truck picked up speed. There was a place they could crash through, a small carved-out niche in the side of the mountain. If he could reach it, they might have a chance at survival.

Just two more hairpin curves. The tires squealed around the first one. The truck leaned on two tires, then fell back to all four.

Liam's heart pounded a painful beat. His pulse echoed in his ears as he readied for the next curve.

He shot Buddy a quick glance, hoping, praying, the dog would be all right when they hit the stand of saplings he planned on aiming for. Taking the chance, he reached over and shoved the dog to the floor. "Stay."

He returned his hand to the steering wheel as they rounded the curve, then yanked it to the right toward the stand of cottonwoods in an area used for turning around. Right before impact, he crossed his arms over his head and leaned into the passenger seat.

The truck groaned as branches slapped the bumper, the hood, smashing the front windshield and raking over the top of the truck. The vehicle hit something else, something immoveable and flipped.

After rolling two times, it stopped upside down. Buddy yelped, weighing Liam down.

Liam put a hand to his head, bringing his hand back bloody. He couldn't move his legs. Because of injury or because of the dog lying on him, he didn't know. Every breath cut like a knife to his side. He groaned and the world grew dark.

Chapter Ten

Kingsley locked up the bank and headed home. The game he'd set in motion, the ruse he'd come up with, kept a smile on his face as he pulled into his garage. His gaze landed on the black bag between the work bench and the wall. Exactly where he'd put it.

Knowing he'd need an explanation for having his fingerprints on the bag, he slipped out of his car, leaving his briefcase on the passenger seat, and opened the bag. Poor Cherie stared up at him with lifeless eyes. Pity she'd had to snoop. He enjoyed her company more than any of the others.

Kingsley called the sheriff's station and reported finding the body, then moved to the kitchen to pour himself a shot of whiskey. He downed the third as the sheriff pulled into his drive.

The stress of the last few weeks showed on the man's face. Kingsley didn't understand the sheriff's popularity. Just because Westbrook was former FBI didn't mean he should be revered. Kingsley had the money and the power; the sheriff had squat. He forced a worried expression onto his face and opened the door. "Thank you for coming."

Westbrook frowned. "It isn't a pleasure call.

Where's the body?"

Straight to the point. "In the garage. Want a drink? I'm so shook up I've had several."

"Not while I'm on duty." He motioned for Kingsley to lead the way.

The sheriff glanced at the car with the driver's door still opened. "In a hurry?"

"I spotted the bag that shouldn't be there. Then…when I saw…her, I raced to the house and called your office. I didn't think about the car." He deserved an Academy Award for his performance.

Westbrook's eyes were slits. "Anyone been here today?"

"Well, my cleaning lady. Oh, and I hired a homeless man, Wilbur, to change some lights that had gone out in the house."

The sheriff scribbled something on a small notepad. He didn't act as if anything Kingsley told him came as a surprise. Kingsley shook the thought off. If the man suspected him, he'd be wearing handcuffs right now.

"Wilbur lives in a tent by the lake. The boat dock on the north side."

"I know where he lives." Westbrook slid the notepad into his pocket. "Excuse me while I have someone secure the scene and take away the body. Do you know the victim?"

He cleared his throat. "Yes. She's…a…uh."

"I know what she is. Was she here when you left this morning?"

"Yes, sir. Sleeping like a baby. Wilbur must have seen her and…"

"Hmm." Westbrook moved past him and onto the front lawn where he placed a call.

The whole visit didn't make sense. The sheriff really acted as if he already knew about Cherie. How could that be? Unless, Miss Gosling was a better actor than Kingsley.

~

Alisa set her bags in the passenger seat of her car and headed to the ranch while singing her favorite shanty at the top of her lungs. She rounded the last of the hairpin curves and slammed on the brakes. Her car fishtailed before coming to a stop. Was that Liam's truck? She pulled over and raced for the navy older-model truck. A whine sounded from under a bush.

"Buddy?" She knelt in the dirt. The dog's leg stuck out at a weird angle. "Liam!" Alisa leaped to her feet and sprinted for the overturned vehicle. "Liam." She peered through the shattered window to a bleeding Liam hanging upside down, secured by his seatbelt.

She reached into the truck and felt for a pulse. There but weak. Where was he injured? "Wake up, Liam." Please, wake up. Alisa yanked on the door, but it wouldn't budge. She retrieved her phone and called 911.

"Is the victim conscious?" The operator asked.

"No, but he is breathing. He's upside down. Should I unbuckle him?"

"No. We don't know his injuries. Help is coming. Stay on the phone."

"We need someone for an injured dog, too."

Alisa spent the time rushing back and forth between Buddy and Liam until the dog dragged his injured leg to her side. She sat, one arm around his neck, and watched the road while keeping up a one-sided conversation with Liam.

"I wish you'd wake up. The ranch isn't going to be

the same without you, and you know you'll be hospitalized. At least for a night." She put her free hand through the window and entwined her fingers with his. "I hope this doesn't hurt. Do you know I'm here?" Tears sprang to her eyes. "I think it's time for us to view the mist over the valley again, don't you? There's no one I'd rather do that with than you. I...really like you, Liam." Maybe more than liked if she were honest.

Finally. She climbed to her feet as Sheriff Westbrook and Deputy Miller pulled up.

"Liam hasn't woken up." She cleared the boulder from her throat that had lodged there the second she spotted the accident. "I think Buddy's leg is broken."

"I'll take this guy to the vet right away. Come on, boy." Miller hefted Buddy into his arms and gently placed him in his backseat. "Ambulance is here. Let O'Ryan know where his dog is when he opens his eyes."

Alisa nodded, her gaze locked on the two paramedics who climbed from the ambulance. "I've been here about an hour, and he hasn't stirred."

"Any idea when the accident occurred?" One of them asked.

"I saw him leave town about thirty minutes before I did, so maybe an hour and a half?" She stepped out of the way as a fire truck blocked the road.

"Over here, Miss Gosling." The sheriff motioned her to his side. "I was at Kingsley's house when I received the call."

"Did you find the woman?"

"I did. He's trying to blame our resident homeless man."

"Why didn't you arrest him?" She crossed her arms and glared.

"There isn't enough evidence yet, but we're getting there. Imagine I'm going to find planted evidence at Wilbur's. I'm hoping I'll find Kingsley's DNA. He'll have trouble convincing me he had a reason to be there."

"Should you be sharing this information?" She arched a brow.

"No." He shrugged. "But, you need to be careful. Sometimes safety trumps doing things by the book."

Her blood chilled. "You don't think Liam's accident was an accident, do you?"

"Liam picked up his truck from the mechanic, then just happens to flip on the most dangerous curve down the mountain. I'd bet my wife's favorite pair of shoes we'll find out his brakes failed."

"Then you can arrest Freddy Jones."

"We can definitely bring him and Bill in for questioning, yes."

She sure hoped the accident hadn't been because someone wanted Liam dead. "I'm the one they should have targeted," she said hoarsely. "I brought trouble here with that cursed letter."

"You brought your share, but Kingsley and Jones were here before you. Don't forget that."

"What if they're tied together? I don't believe in coincidence, but..." She exhaled heavily. "Barker is dead. What if he and Kingsley had ties?"

"You should have been in law enforcement." He smiled. "Because you think like a detective. We're already looking into a connection."

The firemen used the jaws of life to free Liam from the truck, then handed him over to the paramedics who secured him on a gurney. One of them pressed a cloth hard over his thigh.

"The pinning of his leg kept him from bleeding out. We need to get him to the hospital fast." The man glanced at Alisa. "You can follow in your car."

She nodded, her eyes fixed on Liam's overly pale face. "Will he be all right?"

"Too soon to tell."

"Follow me. I can get you there faster." Westbrook strode to his car. "You might want to call the ranch and let his men know."

She nodded and retrieved Liam's phone from the truck. Flipping through the contacts, she found Willy's number.

"Yeah, boss?"

"It's me, Alisa. Liam was in a terrible car accident." Her voice broke. "He's headed to the hospital now. His truck is at the first sharp curve headed up Misty Mountain."

"I'll call a tow truck. Keep us posted, will ya?"

"Yes. Don't take it to Bill's."

"Any particular reason?"

"They were the ones who fixed the brakes on Liam's truck."

"Gotcha."

She hung up and climbed into her car to follow the sheriff to the hospital, praying harder than she ever had before.

~

Liam woke to the beeping of machines. His entire body ached, even his eyelids it seemed. He turned his head slowly to one side.

Alisa, her head at a distorted angle, slept in a chair beside his bed. He was in the hospital.

It all came back to him in a whoosh. His brakes had

failed. The truck had flipped when he'd tried to use a stand of saplings to stop him. "Buddy?"

Alisa jerked upright. "Miller took him to the vet. His leg was knocked out of its socket, but he'll be fine. He was thrown from the truck and fared better than you did."

"What happened to me?"

"The front of the truck resembled a shattered matchbox car. Your leg was pinned. You lost a lot of blood, but the doctor said you'll make a full recovery. Luckily—" she gave a small laugh, "the very debris that kept you in the truck also kept you from bleeding to death."

"Thank God for small favors." He pressed the button to raise the head of his bed. "Are you the one who found me?"

Alisa nodded. "Scared me to death." She went on to tell him of Westbrook's visit with Kingsley.

"The man is going to feel cornered real soon. Then, he'll be even more dangerous."

"The sheriff thinks your brakes—"

"I know the brakes were cut." The sheriff entered the room. "Had the garage in Langley check as soon as the truck arrived. Sorry, Liam, but it's totaled. I've put out an APB on Jones. Bill swears the man is the only one who worked on your vehicle. Now, he can't be found. We found Wilbur. Sure enough, an article of clothing that belonged to Cherie was found in his tent."

"Now what?" Liam shifted, the movement taking his breath away.

"We keep trying to find information on Kingsley. I want to deputize you, O'Ryan. I can use the help, and this way—"

"If he comes for me, you can charge him as if I'm

law enforcement." He chuckled, breaking it off immediately. Laughing, any kind of movement, reminded him how injured he really was.

"Yes. We've also strongly suggested Walt leave town for a while. He finally saw reason when we told him about your accident."

"You'll have to protect Wilbur," Alisa said. "He's a loose end."

"He wasn't at his tent, but we're looking for him. I'm going to have one of my deputies camp outside your hospital room. Little Rock is sending us backup. Miss Gosling, if you're ready, I'd like to follow you to the ranch."

Liam took Alisa's hand. "That's a good idea. How long have you been here?"

"A little over a day. Willy picked up Buddy this morning."

"Good. Stay in the main house for now, please. Buddy will let you know if anyone comes who doesn't belong."

She opened her mouth to protest, then clamped it shut. "Fine."

"I'll be outside when you're ready." The sheriff left them alone.

"Don't worry about anything, Liam." Alisa placed a tender kiss on his cheek. "Between me and your men, we'll take care of the ranch. Even when you're released from here, you won't be doing much."

"You'd be surprised what I can do on crutches." He grinned. "I went deer hunting on them before."

"Why am I not surprised? I'll come by tomorrow." She tossed him a smile and headed for the door. "Be nice to the nurses. You might be here a couple more days."

"Alisa?"

She turned.

"I like you, too."

Chapter Eleven

Kingsley paced his massive master bedroom. Things were unraveling faster than he could keep up with. O'Ryan should be dead, although he wasn't the target. Jones was working on his own agenda. Was he going to have to take care of things himself?

His phone rang. "What?"

"The homeless man is taken care of. Lots of evidence left to suggest he killed Cherie."

"Great. What are you going to do about Miss Gosling?"

Jones cursed. "I thought she would've been in the truck with O'Ryan."

"Idiot. She dropped him off. What was she supposed to do with her vehicle? Fly it back to the ranch? Do the job you're being paid to do." He jammed the off button.

The fool had one more chance to get it right. If he didn't, then Kingsley would get rid of him and clean things up on his own.

~

Alisa waited while Sheriff Westbrook checked out both levels of the main house. Poor Buddy hobbled after him from room to room.

"The main house is clear. I'll check yours out back

and the outlying buildings. Lock the door behind me.”

“Do you really think Jones will come here?”

“Yes, ma’am. Now that things are escalating, it’s only a matter of time. Do you own a gun?”

Icy fingers trailed down her spine. “No. I don’t know how to shoot.”

“You might want to consider learning, ma’am.” He headed for the back door. “Lock your bedroom, too.”

“I will. I’ll be showering, then maybe wind down with a movie before going to bed.” Alisa closed and locked the door after him, then watched him through the window. The man was scaring her. She didn’t think it possible to be more frightened than she was after finding Liam, but now her heart raced.

His flashlight bobbed across the lawn as he made his way to her house. He tried the door, then looked in the windows.

She glanced at Buddy. “That man is overworked. He needs to delegate more. What does his wife think of all the hours he works?” Alisa shook her head and climbed the stairs to take her shower.

Buddy’s tail thumped the floor before he followed her. Alisa closed the door, leaving the dog outside in the hall. She felt safer knowing he’d alert her to any approaching danger. After locking the door, she turned on the shower.

She stood under the spray until the water cooled, letting it wash away the ache from her shoulders and the worry over Liam. He’d be fine, the doctor said. Might even come home in the morning, but she doubted it. The doctor hadn’t looked convinced when Liam asked. Most likely it would be another day or two.

Shower complete, she toweled off and dressed in

cotton pants and a tank top, then opened the door. "I feel like a romantic comedy, Buddy. How about you?" Unfortunately, a search of Liam's movies didn't reveal any. Lots of action and adventure though. "No thank you. I'm living an action movie." She chose to watch a sitcom on television instead.

A car engine roared to life outside. A quick glance showed the sheriff driving away. He must have been very thorough in searching the property.

Willy stood in the driveway watching after the sheriff's car. Seeing Alisa in the window, he waved and headed for the bunkhouse.

The place was as safe and secure as possible. "Let's go to bed." She snapped her fingers for Buddy to follow her to the guestroom where she'd moved his bed earlier. Once inside, she locked her door as she'd promised and climbed into bed.

Growling woke her. It took a few seconds for her to realize Buddy stood at the door.

Swallowing against a sudden dry throat, Alisa focused on hearing what had Buddy worked up. There it was.

A footfall.

The creak of a stair.

Her breath caught. She patted the side of the bed to call Buddy to her side as she slid from under the sheet.

The dog padded to her side. Alisa wrapped her arms around his neck and stared through the night at the bedroom door as she dialed 911.

"911. What's your emergency?"

"Intruder at the Leaning O Ranch," she whispered. "He's outside my bedroom door."

"Is the door locked?"

"Yes."

"Stay there. I'm sending help. Stay on the line."

Instead of staying on the line, she called Willy. "Sorry to wake you, but could you and the guys come over? Someone is in the house."

"Be right there."

She'd done all she could.

Buddy's growls increased.

"Hey!" Someone shouted from downstairs.

Buddy's growls turned to frantic barks as footsteps thundered in the hall. The intruder wasn't risking the stairs.

Alisa raced to the door and flung it open. "He's headed for the attic!"

Willy, gun drawn, gave chase as Deputy Miller stepped into the house. "Stop, Willy. I'll give pursuit. Watch Miss Gosling." The overweight detective clicked on a flashlight and huffed toward the attic stairs.

"You okay?" Willy shot her a glance before staring after the deputy.

"Yes." How did the deputy get there so fast? "Buddy alerted me."

Footsteps overhead, then a loud thump. Willy raced for the stairs, Alisa on his heels.

"Stay behind me." Willy held out an arm.

They slowly entered the attic.

The deputy's flashlight lay on the dust-covered floor. A window on the far side banged against the wall as a night breeze grabbed hold of it. Miller lay next to a pile of boxes.

Alisa rushed to his side. "He's breathing."

Willy glanced out the window. "Whoever was here is gone now. I'll be sleeping on the sofa until the boss returns."

Miller groaned and sat up. "Someone hit me. Did he get away?"

"Yes." Alisa's shoulders sagged. "This is the second time. Whoever this person is, they know this house." Which meant they'd be back. "Willy, I want you to teach me how to shoot. Don't tell Liam about this until he comes home. I'll fill him in then. He doesn't need to worry."

"I can show you tomorrow."

"Don't go all vigilante now." Miller struggled to his feet. "Let us handle this."

"You're doing a right fine job so far." Willy turned and stormed from the attic and down the stairs.

~

Liam had never been gladder to be home despite Alisa's silence after she picked him up. Three days in the hospital were three days too many. He struggled out of her car, leaning heavily on a crutch and hopped to the side so he could close the door. Buddy limped toward him, tail going a mile a minute. "Hey, Buddy. I missed you."

"I think the feeling was mutual." Alisa smiled as she rounded the car. "Come on in. It's lunchtime. The men will be glad to see you."

"Just the men?" He arched a brow.

"Me too." She led the way into the house and to the kitchen where several boxes of pizza lay open on the table.

His men grinned and clapped, shouting out welcome backs.

"It ain't the same, boss," Willy said. "Miss Alisa here isn't near as bossy as you. We rattled around like pebbles in a tin can."

"Sure, you did." He sat in a chair. He knew his men would do their jobs whether he was here or not. "Any trouble while I was gone?"

The men glanced at each other, then Alisa seemed to be overly interested in the pizza.

"What happened?" Liam narrowed his eyes in Alisa's direction.

She bit her bottom lip, a gesture that made his stomach flutter. "Uh, we had an intruder again. I called 911 and Willy. Deputy Miller arrived, very quickly in fact, as did Willy. The deputy was hit over the head and the intruder escaped out the attic window. That's it."

"That's it?" He scowled. "Why wasn't I told?" He glared at Willy.

"Because I asked that it wait until you came home." Alisa hitched her chin. "You couldn't do anything from the hospital anyway."

"Men, take the pizza outside." Liam slid one box closer to him. "I need to speak with Miss Gosling." The men filed out.

"So, it's Miss Gosling now?" Her cheeks reddened.

"When I'm talking to you as an employee, it is. Why wasn't I told?"

"Why bother you in the hospital?"

"Because it's my house."

"What could you have done?"

"Come home." He slapped the tabletop.

A sly smile teased at her lips. "My point exactly."

The woman infuriated him. "You overstepped—"

Willy poked his head into the kitchen. "Boss?"

"What?"

"The sheriff wants to talk to you."

"Send him in." He was seeing way too much of Sheriff Westbrook.

The sheriff entered the kitchen. Weary lines creased his face. "I'm going to take a long vacation after this is all over. Miss Gosling, you okay?"

"I'm fine. Miller?"

"Mild concussion." He exhaled heavily. "I stopped by to tell you we found Wilbur floating in Misty Lake with a bullet hole between his eyes."

"That takes away him being the one who killed Cherie." Liam shook his head. "Why kill the one person keeping Kingsley from being accused?"

"I'll tell you as soon as you're a deputy." The sheriff swore him in and handed him a badge.

"I'm not sure how much good I'll be with a bum leg."

"Just doing my best to protect you. Your primary job is to keep watch over Miss Gosling. Keep your eyes and ears open. Eventually you'll get a positive ID on the person who keeps paying you a visit. When you do, we'll know who to arrest."

"Any sign of Jones?"

The sheriff shook his head. "Vanished."

Liam stared at the badge on the table as Alisa took a slice of pizza and sat. "What if we're right about Kingsley, and I'm pretty certain we are, and there's someone out there who wants to take over his operation?" He asked. "That's the best explanation for getting rid of Wilbur that I can think of."

"Makes sense to me." The sheriff shrugged. "May I?" He motioned to the pizza.

"Help yourself." Liam folded his arms. "Kingsley has been the bank manager for ten years. It's only recently that we've had the drugs and prostitution. What is the attraction in Misty Hollow? Small town, not a lot of prospects."

"Slipping under the radar," Alisa said. "The drugs and prostitution were here at the snap of a finger. There's no competition in a small town, and we're thirty minutes away from two larger cities. It's the perfect place."

"I think you're right." The sheriff pulled up a chair. "My wife and her mother came here in the Witness Protection Program. They aren't anymore. The man responsible is behind bars and my wife and her mother are very wealthy women. We've had others who came to hide or start over. Misty Hollow had been untainted for so long no one considered that crime could reach this town. It's not exactly on the beaten path."

"How does your wife put up with your late hours?" Alisa tilted her head.

"She stays busy between here and New York. Her father used to…well, is…Anthony Bartelloni, crime boss. He's in prison right now."

"So, it's all in a day's work?"

"Yep." He grinned and pushed to his feet. "Liam, sorry to say this, but you'll need to accompany Miss Gosling when she goes to clean houses. Other than that, be careful and don't deviate from your normal schedule. Somebody in this town knows about who is responsible for these deaths. I want to know who that somebody is." He stood. "Have you learned to shoot?"

"Yes. Willy taught me and gave me a gun."

"You have a gun?" Liam's heart skipped a beat.

"Yep. Turns out I'm a pretty good shot, too."

Liam sighed and prayed she'd never have to use it on a human being. He added himself to that prayer. He'd need to start carrying. Not that it would have stopped the accident. What scared him the most, though, was the fact that he and Alisa would always be together. Take out one of them, and you took out both. Not a scenario he liked.

Chapter Twelve

Liam did not look happy about clunking up Mrs. Mayfield's sidewalk on his crutch. Nor was he happy about leaving Buddy behind. His griping on the drive into town had given her a headache.

He might be reluctant to sit around, but Alisa's client was ecstatic. "I brought you company while I clean." She flashed a grin over her shoulder.

Liam's smile looked pained. "I'm…"

They'd never discussed what they would tell people. "He can't do anything much around the ranch so decided to tag along and see how I spend my days."

"That's wonderful." The old woman clapped her hands together. "I'll pour another cup of tea."

"I spend half an hour visiting first," Alisa said as the woman bustled away. "Makes for a longer day, but it means a lot to her."

"You've a kind heart."

She put a hand to her chest. "Thank you. My grandmother always said kindness was classy."

"I agree." He made his way to the kitchen table and took a seat, leaning his crutches against the wall. "Chocolate chip cookies?"

"Either these or oatmeal. I come twice a week, and

she alternates." Alisa leaned closer and whispered, "I suspect she freezes whatever is left over."

He chuckled, bad mood apparently dispelled at the sight of cookies. "There won't be any leftovers today."

Alisa left her supplies on the stairs out of the way and then snagged a cookie and sat at the table. "It doesn't take me long to clean since I don't go upstairs."

"A whirling dervish, this one." Mrs. Mayfield tsked. "Here and gone before I get used to someone else in the house."

"Don't complain. You're the only one who's home while I'm cleaning. I prefer the house to be empty." Alisa smiled.

"So you can snoop." She winked at Liam.

"No!" Well, she did intend to do a little looking around at Mr. Kingsley's house that afternoon.

"You don't peek into medicine cabinets or drawers left open just a smidge?" She held her thumb and forefinger a hair's breadth apart. "Oh, I'm just teasing you."

"Very funny." They chitchatted about the town's residents for a few minutes. Since Liam was there to entertain the woman, Alisa finished sooner than expected.

"I've some time before heading to Mr. Kingsley's house," she said. "Anywhere you need to go, Liam?"

"Lunch at the diner. Before that, I've a prescription that needs filling for antibiotics. I also need a new truck. Older model. If you don't mind driving me to the farm, that would be great."

Alisa glanced at the clock on the wall. "Would going out to the farm after Kingsley's place work?"

"I'm at your mercy." He held his hands out. "I go

where you go."

Mrs. Mayfield cleared the empty cookie plate from the table. "Enjoy it, dear. I wish I had a handsome man tagging along after me."

"He's only along because of his leg. Believe me, he'd rather be working his ranch." Alisa laughed. "I could send Willy over. He's younger, so that would make you a cougar."

"Oh, hush. The things you say." The old woman blushed. "See you in a few days."

Still laughing, Alisa followed Liam from the house. Minutes later, she pulled in front of the drugstore. "Unless you need me, I'll wait here."

"No need to come." He thumped his way into the store.

Alisa pulled up "What Do You Do with a Drunken Sailor" on her Bluetooth and cranked up the speaker, belting out the lyrics. After a few odds looks tossed her way, she lowered the volume on the speaker and her voice.

"Shave his belly with a rusty razor?" Liam smirked as he opened the car door.

She turned off the song and shrugged. "I enjoy sea shanties."

"I would never have guessed that." He slid in. "We could walk to the diner, but then I'd have to toss this crutch."

Five minutes later they sat in a booth in the crowded diner. Liam ordered chicken fried steak, potatoes, and fried okra.

"I cannot believe you're that hungry after all those cookies." Alisa handed her menu to the waitress. "Chef salad, please." She glanced around the room. "There's

Walt's friend." The man looked lonely. "It was those two who got me started on the Kingsley thing." She really wished they hadn't, but she wished a lot of things. Like not finding that paper. Alisa glanced up at Liam. But then she wouldn't have rented a house from him. There were no regrets there. Everything would be perfect if she hadn't been followed.

"Why are you frowning?" Liam reached across the table and put a hand over hers.

"This whole thing. I know why I'm in danger, but why you?"

"Jones hates me for firing him. Promised to get even. Guess he did." He motioned to his leg, then lowered his voice. "I stayed up a while last night checking the internet for anything related to Kingsley, Barker Construction, and the state's organized crime."

"And?" Anticipation sprouted like a seed.

"The big guy in the state is a Richard Preston. Further digging revealed the groundbreaking photo for Barker Construction. Guess who is in the picture?"

"Preston?"

"And Kingsley who happened to be standing shoulder to shoulder with Preston."

"The three know each other." One step closer. "I found that letter, turned it in...oh." She widened her eyes. "No one knew I had that letter before coming here except for the cop who took it from me."

"A dirty cop. One who notified his boss, and I'm not talking at the station."

"Preston or Kingsley. The bank manager would have known right away that I came here. I simply picked the wrong town to relocate in." She crossed her arms and sat against the back of the booth. "We need to tell the sheriff our theory."

"We'll go right after lunch."

~

Sheriff Westbrook smiled when they finished telling him their deductions. "I've said it before. You two would seriously make good law enforcement. We've seen the photo. It's one more piece of the mountain of evidence against Kingsley."

Liam shook his head. "You haven't arrested Kingsley yet because you're hoping he'll lead you to Preston?"

The sheriff didn't even look ashamed by his deceit. "Guilty. You're intelligent enough to know that I can't tell you all the details of an active investigation, even if you're deputized."

"We're headed to Kingsley's when we leave here. Anything you want us to look for?"

"Nothing. I don't want either of you to be discovered and turn up like Cherie."

Aha. "She was killed for snooping?"

"We believe so. One of the other girls met up with Miller and told him Cherie said she was going to make some big money by locating some information. Didn't say from whom or where she'd find that information."

"Caught and killed." Alisa's knuckles whitened as she folded her hands in her lap.

Liam took her hand. Her grip loosened at his touch. "So, no snooping. I'm good with that." He'd also find a subtle way to let Kingsley know he'd been deputized. Not that it would deter the man from killing him, but it might make him think twice first. "Any sign of Jones?"

"No, but there are a hundred places a body could hide on this mountain. I've alerted the park rangers to be on the lookout. We need all the help we can get."

"Since we now know Preston is involved, will the FBI be called in?"

"Most likely. I've contacted a buddy of mine in Quantico. He'll get back to me soon."

Liam lumbered to his feet. "Thanks." Outside, he turned to Alisa. "While it makes me feel good that we come to the same conclusions as the sheriff's department, it irks me that he doesn't fill us in until we come to him with what he already knows."

"Active investigation." She reached for the car door.

"If we all worked together, I wouldn't waste my time on information already revealed." Liam slid into the car, almost whacking Alisa in the head with his crutch as he dropped it in the backseat. "Sorry."

"Leg hurting? You're kind of grouchy again."

"Yes, but that doesn't make me grouchy."

"Oh, but you are so wrong." She grinned and pulled the car away from the curb.

"Drat. He's here." She jerked her chin toward the house.

Kingsley waved from the front porch.

"He already knows we're here, plus he's expecting you." He shoved open the door as Kingsley's smile faded at the sight of him

. "Good afternoon." Liam grinned and thumped his way onto the porch. "Hope you don't mind if I sit right here and wait on Alisa."

"Of course not, although I do find it strange that you're dragging after her."

"Can't do much at the ranch with this bum leg." Liam fell back onto a rocking chair. "Pretend I'm not here." He shifted to pull his badge from the back pocket of his jeans and opened it right before Kingsley entered the house.

The man gave a tiny gasp, then slammed the door.

Liam's grin widened as he pushed with his foot to set the rocker in motion. Now, word would spread that Liam had been deputized, at least for a short time. Hopefully, the fact would keep Alisa safe until the guys could be locked up.

How much more information did Westbrook need? If Kingsley knew Preston, then he was most likely the kingpin's plant here. Why had it taken Kingsley all this time of living in Misty Hollow before bringing in the crime? Were they that patient about someone settling into the community first?

~

Kingsley didn't care that O'Ryan was a deputy. It wouldn't stop him from making sure Miss Gosling didn't cause trouble over that cursed letter. Though she didn't seem to think he was involved. She moved about the house bobbing her head to whatever tune came from her earbuds. If she knew about Cherie—that he'd ordered Jones to torch Barker Construction—she'd cancel cleaning his house.

The thought relaxed him a bit. He sat in his leather recliner and stared out the window. Why was O'Ryan really here? Kingsley turned his gaze back to Miss Gosling.

It seemed suspicious that a man who'd almost died from an accident mere days ago would accompany her while she cleaned houses. Bored or not, he'd sit on the front porch for more than an hour. Torture for an active man like him. Kingsley rose to his feet and watched as O'Ryan rocked back and forth, his gaze on the road.

"What are you doing here?"

"Did you say something?" Miss Gosling removed an earbud.

"No, just thinking out loud." He pasted on a smile.

"I didn't expect you to be here." She tilted her head.

"A bit of a stomach bug, I think." He rubbed his stomach. "Thought I could use a quiet day at home."

"I'll hurry so you can be alone." She carried her supplies upstairs.

O'Ryan never stopped rocking, never stopping watching the road. It was starting to grate on Kingsley's nerves. He paced the living room, doubt again clouding his mind about why the man had come. Intimidation? But why? Again, no one knew who he was or what he'd done.

Sure, the sheriff came back after Wilbur was found, but Kingsley had an alibi that night. He'd been seen working late at the bank.

Idiot Jones. Someone needed to stop him before he ruined everything.

Chapter Thirteen

It being Sunday, Alisa found herself torn between a trip to watch the mist dissipate or a horse ride. When she brought it up to Liam, he discouraged her.

"You're safer sticking around the ranch." He glanced out the window. "It's still dark and too dangerous."

"Then I'll wait until daylight and go riding. I won't go far." She scrambled eggs into a large bowl for the men's breakfast while bacon sizzled in the pan. A simple and fast meal so she could enjoy her day off. "I want to head to the creek with my book. I'll take the walkie-talkie and my gun. And don't worry, I'll be fine."

"If you go just a bit past the clearing by the creek, you'll find a very old graveyard with about twenty graves. My father said it might be the first settlers on this mountain, but there's no sign of a church ever being there. It's super creepy at night." He laughed. "Don't go past the barbed-wire fence, okay? My land extends past that, but I'll worry if you're too far away. I'm no good to you with one good leg."

"I promise not to go more than a mile." Alisa had no idea how far a mile was. "Or the graveyard, whichever is farther." She flipped the bacon and rang the bell for the morning meal.

After everyone ate and she'd finished the dishes, having declined Liam's help since he'd have to prop himself on the crutch, Alisa changed into jeans, packed a book, a water bottle, and a granola bar, then headed outside. She intended to stay gone all day. Now that she stayed in the main house at night, total solitude became rare. Alisa really needed some alone time.

As she reached the main doors leading into the barn, she started to insert her earbuds but stopped when an angry voice came from inside. The door hung open a few inches. Alisa halted. Should she go in or make a noise to alert the man inside that she was there? She started to clear her throat when he said her name.

"I'm telling you Alisa doesn't know anything. I've been in the house twice. If she knew anything, knew that she's the target, do you think she'd stick around?"

A few seconds of silence.

"I'm not going in again. Last time I almost got caught. Had to hit Miller over the head. Get someone else. Find Jones and make him do your dirty work."

Buddy barked from the direction of the house, cutting off the conversation in the barn.

If she didn't do something quick, he'd find her. "Not this time, boy." She walked with heavy footsteps to the door. "Stay with Liam." Her steps froze. "Oh, hello, Lars."

"Need any help?"

"No, I uh…" she backed from the barn and rushed back to the house.

She'd have to tell Liam about overhearing Lars' side of a conversation Catching him sleeping, she decided to wait until later. She really wanted, needed, that horseback ride. She watched out the window until Lars left the barn and climbed into a work truck. Once he'd left the ranch, Alisa rushed to the barn to ready her horse.

Her pack secured behind, Alisa swung onto the saddle and headed out the back doors of the barn. The tension she'd been holding in slipped away the further she rode.

Soon, the babbling of the creek over rocks reached her ears. Alisa continued riding until she spotted the first weathered tombstone. She slid from Sadie and looped the reins around the saddle horn so the horse could graze while she strolled the moss-covered graveyard.

Birds chirped from the trees overhead.

Alisa ran her hand over the rough surface of a tombstone that simply said Alice, the rest of the words long since erased by time and weather. Oh, if only the stones could talk. The stories they'd tell.

A twig snapped off to her right.

Sadie nickered.

"Hello?"

When no further sound came and the horse returned to her grazing, Alisa continued her stroll. When she'd reached the last one, overgrown with weeds, she sighed deeply wishing for peace to be restored. Smiling, she climbed into the saddle and headed back to the creek.

Her neck prickled shortly after she settled against a tree and opened her book. She glanced at Sadie, her ears twitching as she stared into the trees across the creek.

The horse didn't seem alarmed, so Alisa turned her attention back to the serial killer mystery in her hands. When another twig snapped, pulling her away from the story, she gave up and slapped her book closed.

She nibbled at the granola bar, drank some of her

water, and climbed on the horse to head back. Some kind of critter seemed overly curious about her. Bears and coyotes lived on the mountain, and she had no desire to run into one of them.

A glance over her shoulder revealed a shadow moving through the trees. A shadow that looked suspiciously like a man.

Had she been followed? Was it Lars or Jones?

Her heart beat erratically, thumping against her ribcage. Her mouth dried despite the recent drink of water. She nudged Sadie into a trot.

~

Good help was definitely hard to find no matter how much they were paid. Avery was the second man this week to disobey a direct order.

Kingsley called Preston from the burner phone and explained the situation. "Can you send me someone I can trust? Someone who will follow orders without hesitation?"

"I have two I'll send. They'll be new employees at the garage by the end of tomorrow. I want this finished, Kingsley. If I could risk it, I'd come settle things myself. As it is, France is now my home. Toss this phone and buy another one." Click.

Was that an order to dispose of Gosling and O'Ryan? Kingsley slipped the phone into his pocket. He'd toss it in the lake on his way home from work. In the meantime, it was daily routine as usual. His boss wasn't the only one who couldn't draw too much attention. Things in Misty Hollow were heating up.

As if the heat had seeped into the air-conditioned bank, he tugged at his collar, then straightened his tie. For the first time since taking the job as bank manager, he felt claustrophobic.

~

"You're back earlier than I thought." Liam muted the action movie on the TV.

"I'm being careful." She plopped onto the sofa next to him. "Someone was following me. It started at the graveyard. Were any of the men gone for a while?"

"I don't know. I spent time doing the books in my office, then chilled in front of the TV." He took one look at her and knew she wasn't telling him something. "Okay, spill."

"I overheard a conversation between Lars and someone else. I'm definitely the target. They've always known about that letter. Lars also said he's the one coming into the house." She picked at the fringe on a throw pillow. "What I don't understand is why they haven't killed me yet?"

He glanced at her with concern. They'd had plenty of opportunity. "They think you have something."

"But I only found that one letter."

Liam turned off the movie. "Let's pay the sheriff another visit. We're missing something." He stood and reached for his crutch. "Sorry about your non-restful Sunday. You should have told me right away about Lars." Why did she hold onto dangerous information?

"Because you would've stopped me from taking a ride."

True.

"I'll still go riding, Liam. I'm not going to stay inside like a prisoner." She set her chin in a determined pose. "They haven't attempted to kill me yet, so until they realize I don't have anything else, I plan on living. You're the only one they tried to kill." An emotion flickered across her face that led him to believe she didn't believe the words she spoke. Why be so stubborn?

"Pretty sure that was Jones acting on his promise of revenge. I don't think it pertains to this situation at all." He followed her to her car. "Will you at least consider my request?"

Why couldn't she understand he was trying to keep her safe? Liam liked having her in the big house, and for the first time, he hated rattling around in it by himself. Not only did he enjoy her company, Liam liked seeing her face. Talking to her.

"What?" She glanced over at him as she drove away from the house. "And, yes, I'll consider staying close to the ranch."

He smiled. "Has anyone ever told you how beautiful you are?"

"Yes. My father." A smile teased at her lips. "He said I was the most gorgeous thing he'd ever seen."

Liam agreed. "The man had good eyes."

She blushed and pressed her lips together, returning her attention to the road. "So, what are you going to do about Lars?"

"Fire him, most likely." Finding someone to replace him would be difficult. Not too many young men wanted to live on a ranch, work long days, and have little time off no matter how good the pay.

They sat in the sheriff's office, waiting for him to return from a meeting with the police sent down from Little Rock.

"Now that help has arrived, this should all be over soon." Alisa turned around a photo on the desk. "The sheriff's wife is pretty. Love the red hair."

Liam preferred Alisa's dark hair and eyes which

gave her an exotic look. "I haven't met her. They live up on the mountain. Her mother handles things in New York, I believe."

"You know a lot for not having met her."

"Word travels fast in a small town, remember?"

"Sorry to make you wait." The sheriff rushed into the room. "Tell me what you have quick. I'm not finished briefing the loaned officers."

Alisa gave a recount of Lars' phone call. Hearing the words again of how she was the target wrenched his gut.

"So, it's obvious from that call that Lars and Jones are involved. My guess is that Lars was talking to Kingsley on the phone."

"Do you have enough evidence now?" Alisa leaned forward.

"I believe so. Good work, you two. Stay safe." He hurried away.

"Well, now I have the unpleasant task of firing Lars." The man was a good ranch hand, too.

"Want me to come with you?" Alisa asked when they returned home.

"No. I'm still trying to come up with a reason to fire him without letting him know you overheard him." And he drew a complete blank.

"That is a hard one. Do you have to fire him? I mean, we know he's the one who entered the house. We can keep a closer eye on him, have Willy help."

That would keep Lars from being suspicious, which in turn would make Preston and Kingsley feel the same. "Okay. We'll leave it for now."

Rather than go into the house, he headed for the barn despite Alisa's protests that he should sit back on the sofa. Liam needed to think, and the best way he could do that was to curry his horse. Besides, he hadn't been doing any work the last few days and needed to make sure that things were as they should be. If he was really lucky, he'd find a good reason to let Lars go.

Speaking of the man, Lars was mucking stalls in the barn and gave Liam a nod of acknowledgment.

"Going to start working again?" Lars asked.

"Not until I can stand on both legs. I don't mind the crutch, but to work I need to stand straight. I'm just here to spend some time with Lloyd." The big gray horse nickered a welcome. "The boarded horses getting regular exercise?"

"Yes, sir. Between the three of us, we're keeping things running along pretty good. Could use you back, though."

So many questions Liam wanted to ask, like what were they looking for?

Chapter Fourteen

Kingsley saw the sheriff coming just in time to flee out the back of the bank. It didn't take a genius to figure out that the sheriff and two deputies coming his way were trouble. Time to go into hiding until a new plan, a new life, could be arranged.

"It's been fun, Misty Hollow. Adios." He sped toward his house. Through the rearview mirror, he watched as those chasing him jumped into their vehicles and followed.

All he needed was what was in his safe. It would only take seconds.

He didn't stop to turn off the car. Kingsley darted in the house and made a beeline for the safe in the master closet. Clamoring down the back stairs and out the kitchen door, he headed to the car waiting in a back building. Pulling a revolver from the holster under his suit jacket, he ran.

Sheriff Westbrook came around the corner of the house and took aim.

Kingsley fired.

The sheriff spun and dropped. Good riddance.

Kingsley jumped into the waiting car and raced down the road away from Misty Hollow. Let Preston's new goons handle things from now on. "I shot the sheriff, but I did not shoot the deputy." He laughed.

~

"I have to go to the sheriff's office." Liam glanced up from his phone. "I'm being called in."

"What does that mean?" Alisa turned away from the stove.

"The sheriff was shot chasing Kingsley to his house. Miller is in control and calling in all deputies, even volunteers." He eyed the crutch against the wall, no longer needing it. A limp was better than a crutch.

Alisa paled. "Is the sheriff dead?"

"No, but he'll be out of commission for a while. That's all I know right now. I'll fill you in later." Liam climbed to his feet and took a careful step. Not unbearable. He'd be fine.

"Be careful." Worry creased her brow.

"I'll have Willy keep an eye on you while I'm gone." He grabbed his gun and truck keys. "Try not to leave the house."

He hated leaving her, but he'd taken on the role of deputy, believing his only concern would be Alisa. While he could step down from volunteering, the department needed able-bodied men with good minds. Liam could help.

He turned around and gathered Alisa in his arms, resting his chin on her head. "Stay safe." He closed his eyes and breathed in the lemony-scented shampoo she used. The sheriff being shot brought the danger closer. Stepping outside could mean the same for Liam or Alisa.

"You do the same." She gave him a squeeze and stepped back. "Don't be a hero."

"There you go. Taking away my dream." He planted

a quick kiss on her cheek before he changed his mind, then limped as fast as possible to his vehicle.

As he passed Bill's Garage, he spotted two men he didn't recognize. The mechanic hadn't wasted any time replacing Jones. Now, Kingsley had fled town.

The sheriff's department buzzed with activity. Liam wasn't the only civilian Westbrook had deputized. He'd also done the same with Spencer Thorne who had seen his share of trouble in Misty Hollow. "Hey, Spence. How's the sheriff?"

"Hey. He's in surgery. The bullet took him in the gut." He frowned. "Should you be off crutches?"

"With the work we'll need to do, they'll be a hindrance. What's the word?" Liam crossed his arms and watched as the receptionist, dried mascara on her cheeks, darted from the conference to her desk and back again.

"Not sure. Miller popped out long enough to tell me to wait here for you."

"Me?" Liam shrugged. "Bet he's going to send us up the mountain to look for Kingsley."

"Most likely, and we both know he won't hide up there. He'll think he's too good for a cave or a hunter's cabin. I've had the owner tear down the one that bad guys always seem drawn to. They'll have to go further to find something else."

Sure enough, Miller finally graced them with his presence and told them to scour every road on the mountain. "Thorne, you know the area like your backyard. If he's up there, you'll find him. He's in a new vehicle. Dark sedan, Mercedes, I think."

"The mountain is my back door, but no, I don't think he's up there."

"Look anyway. I can't have a couple of volunteer

deputies going over evidence at Kingsley's house or office. If we weren't short-handed, I'd take those badges and send you on your way. What was Westbrook thinking?" He shook his head and marched away.

"Westbrook knew that if anything happened to him, Miller would be in charge," Spence said.

"Which means he didn't have faith in Miller's ability to run things. That's why he deputized us. Because he knew we're the best he has." The idea filled Liam with pride. "So, we pretend we're going up the mountain, but we'll do what we think is best. What's Miller going to do? Fire us?"

"That sounds like a good plan." Spence clapped him on the shoulder. "Let's check the closest motels. If we don't find him, we'll start searching further. Hopefully, there aren't too many dark Mercedes around."

Driving around would allow Liam to rest his leg. They asked for anyone matching Kingsley's description at the two motels between Misty Hollow and Langley and came up empty.

"How far do you think he'll have gone?" Spence asked.

"I'd wager he left the county."

"Or the state."

"Let's switch gears and focus on Jones. Since he's low on the food chain, he'll have stayed close. One of my ranch hands, whom I don't trust by the way, is friends with him. He wouldn't mind hiding out in a hunting cabin. Let's not forget Jones lived here before, so he might have family property."

"Time to involve the women." Spence grinned. "They'll find out faster than anyone whether Jones has land around here."

~

Liam came home with a man named Spencer Thorne and his wife, Sierra.

Alisa glanced at the stew on the stove. It should be enough for two more people. "Have a seat. Supper's done."

"Actually, you and Sierra will be eating at the diner tonight," Liam said, grinning. "In fact, the two of you should leave now."

Alisa crooked a brow but said okay and fetched her purse from her room. Liam must have a reason for secrecy.

Once in the car, Sierra filled her in.

"Why wouldn't Miller want his help?" That didn't make sense. "Unless he thinks they'll do a better job than him. Or—" She snapped her fingers. "He's afraid they'll find out something about him."

"That's a stretch but a possibility." Sierra laughed. "Our mission tonight is to figure out whether Jones's family owns any property around these parts."

"Makes you feel like a secret agent, doesn't it?" Alisa returned her smile, feeling as if she'd made a good friend. "Here's our suspect list. Kingsley, Preston, Jones, and the ranch hand, Avery. Jones and Avery are good friends. He might know about property."

"If he's in cahoots with Jones, he won't spill any information."

True. If Alisa had ever mastered the art of flirting, she might have succeeded at coercing information from Avery.

"Spencer told me you found a letter from someone threatening to expose someone else. If you don't have the information anymore, why are you still in danger?"

Alisa gave a quick shrug. "Maybe they think I have something else. I don't, but that's the only theory we could come up with."

Turns out they were in luck. Walt had returned to the diner.

"Sir, may my friend and I buy you supper?" Alisa asked, motioning her head toward Sierra.

"Mrs. Thorne. It's good to see you in town," Walt said. "Sure. I'd be a fool to turn down the company of a couple of pretty gals. See ya." He clapped his friend on the shoulder and followed Alisa to a table away from the other diners. "So, what do you want to know this time? I heard Kingsley skipped town. I was right, wasn't I?"

"You sure were." Alisa slid into the booth after Sierra. "Is that why you came back from wherever you deemed safe?"

"Yep. I don't like staying away long." He waved the waitress over. "Switch my food over here. The ticket, too."

She nodded and glanced at Alisa. "What will you have?"

"I'll take the salmon special."

"Same," Sierra said. "Might as well make the men pay for sending us out. Do you know Freddy Jones?"

Walt's nose curled. "Not on an empty stomach, please."

"Come on. It gives us something to do while we wait for our food." Sierra wiggled her brows.

"First, you tell me how the sheriff is doing. Heard Spence is a deputy."

"For now, anyway. The sheriff is out of surgery and expected to make a full recovery. Won't be at work for a while. Now talk." She lowered her voice in a playful attempt at barking an order.

"You know, Miss Alisa, Sierra here came to town with trouble on her heels once. Spence protected her. Now, they're married. I'm willing to bet the same with you and O'Ryan." He cackled. "Happened to the sheriff, too. A damsel in distress, a few murders, and then a wedding."

Alisa's face heated. "I work for Liam, nothing more."

"If you say so. Oh, look, our food."

"You're stalling, Walt." Sierra shook her head.

"The Joneses were spit poor. Are you still going to pay for my supper?" He wasted no time digging into a plate of meatloaf, mashed potatoes, and green beans.

Alisa sighed and cut into her salmon. "So, they didn't own any property where Jones could hide out. Another dead end."

"Well, the Jones family didn't own anything, but Mrs. Jones's family—that would be Freddy's mother—did."

Alisa perked up. "Where?"

"A duplex in Langley, a couple cabins they rent out by the lake…" He touched his chin, "and the house here in town Jones was staying in."

"Addresses?"

"You'd have to get them from the po-lice. Of course, the department won't work right with Miller in charge." He leaned over the table and lowered his voice. "That deputy is dirty to the bone. Mark my words, he's on Kingsley's payroll. You'll see."

His gut wasn't wrong before. "You've just earned your supper." Alisa smiled. This information would give Liam and Spencer something to work with. "Heard anything more about what's happening to this town?"

"Besides going to Hades on a speeding train? The working ladies don't stand on the street corners, at least. They must find their clients in other ways. The drug-dealing punks hang around the park. Can't wait until the sheriff cleans up this town."

"You sound like an old western movie." Sierra took the receipt the waitress left on the table. "But you, old man, are worth every one of the ten dollars that meatloaf costs me. Be careful, okay? You're a fixture in this town."

As they drove home, the women tossed around ideas of what Preston and his men thought Alisa knew. "Too bad that building burned down," Alisa said. "I'd go back and figure out why they haven't killed me yet."

Sierra cut her a sharp glance. "Let's hope they don't get tired of waiting."

Chapter Fifteen

Alisa bolted upright in bed and glanced at the clock on her bedside table. Four a.m. She'd been dreaming about the last time she'd cleaned at Barker Construction. When she'd found that horrible letter that started all this.

She'd left her cart in the hall, taking only the cleaning supplies she needed into Barker's office. What if whoever had been on the other side of the door while she hid slipped something in with her supplies? Something they didn't want to be caught with?

She put on slippers and left her room, trying not to wake Liam.

"What's up?" He flicked on his light as she tiptoed past.

"Sorry to wake you. I had a dream and…" He would think her crazy if she told him.

"Want something to drink?" He tossed aside his blanket and limped to her side. "I wasn't sleeping well anyway."

"Sure, but I want to check something first. I'll meet you in the kitchen." She rushed outside to her car and opened her trunk. Where would someone hide something? Not in any of the bottles.

What did she still have from that night? Most of her supplies had run out and been replaced.

Her gaze landed on her extra pair of gloves. Pink with a zebra-striped band around the top. Heart in her throat, she pulled them from the corner of the crate she kept her things in and felt each finger. Something hard in the left index finger. She pulled out a flash drive.

"What are you doing?"

She screamed and whipped around, then punched Liam in his arm. "You scared me."

"Ow." He rubbed his arm. "Sorry, but why are you out here in the dark alone?"

"I thought of something. Come inside. I'll show you." She jogged back to the house and retrieved her laptop from her room. By the time she set the items on the kitchen table, Liam had come in.

"My dream was about that night in Barker's office. I'd left my cart in the hall. I dreamed someone dropped something into my cart." Alisa inserted the thumb drive into the computer. "I found this flash drive in my extra pair of gloves." She moved aside to give Liam room to see the screen.

"Those look like bank records." Liam said. "There's Preston's name."

His close proximity made it difficult for Alisa to concentrate. Why did he smell so good so early in the morning, and why hadn't he put a shirt on? "And names. Do you think these are the people who work for Preston?" She glanced up, her face dangerously close to his lips.

"Whatever it is, we shouldn't have it. Too dangerous." His gaze dropped to her mouth.

"We can turn it over," she whispered.

"To the sheriff." His head lowered.

"Right. Not Miller." She closed her eyes. He was going to kiss her.

Gentle at first, then harder when she returned the kiss. Liam cupped the back of her head and pulled her closer, his kisses heating up. His lips trailed over her cheek and down her neck until she thought she'd stop breathing. When he finally returned his lips to hers, she'd forgot what they were doing.

Liam chuckled and moved his hand to her cheek as he raised his head. "I've been wanting to do that for a long time. Didn't expect it to be right after finding something we shouldn't."

She cleared her throat. "The sheriff is still at the hospital. With your badge, they'll let us see him." Why couldn't she tear her gaze away from his? No one had ever kissed her with such tenderness and roughness at the same time.

"Let's get dressed. I'll buy you breakfast after we turn this over."

She nodded, eyeing his strong back as he limped away. Before getting up from the table, she copied the files onto her laptop, then hid the laptop between the mattresses on the side of the bed she didn't sleep on.

Once she was dressed, hair pulled back from her face and a spritz of perfume on her neck, the flash drive went into the pocket of her jeans. It felt hot, a constant burning reminder that she needed to get rid of it as soon as possible.

Liam waited near the front door, petting Buddy, a faraway look on his face. He smiled and glanced up as she came down the stairs. "After breakfast, Spence and I are going to check out some places where Jones might be hiding. Want to come along? It's better than leaving you here by yourself."

She did a quick mental check of her to-do list. "Sure. I have one house to clean if you don't mind me doing that before we go."

"Not at all." He held the door open for her, leaning in to sniff her neck. "You smell like flowers."

Her face heated. "Thanks. Gardenia." Mercy. She hurried to the car and slid in the driver's seat.

Liam grinned and dangled a set of car keys in front of her. "I'm driving."

Right. No crutch, not that it should have mattered. It was his left leg that had been injured. She exited her car and climbed into his truck. "I still think you're pushing your injury too far."

"I'm fine. I sit whenever I can." He reached over and gave her hand a squeeze, his gaze warm.

That kiss had changed everything. They no longer felt like employer and employee, landlord and tenant. So, what were they?

~

Wow. That kiss. Liam had plans on doing a lot of kissing with Alisa. He smiled and pulled into the hospital parking lot. They'd made the drive in comfortable silence, giving Liam plenty of time to dwell on what had just happened.

Instead of walking ahead of him like she'd done that morning after finding the drive, Alisa slowed her pace to match his. She slipped her hand in his without saying a word.

Warmth flooded through him at the simple gesture. Maybe he wouldn't have to find out what living without Alisa would be like.

He flashed his badge at the nurse's station. They didn't blink an eye at his request to see the sheriff. Liam would miss the badge when this was all over, and he returned to simply being a ranch owner.

The sheriff's eyes opened when they entered. "This can't be good." He winced as he raised his bed to a sitting position.

"I found this in my cleaning supplies." Alisa handed him the drive. "Someone shoved it inside a glove with my cleaning supplies when I cleaned Barker's office. It looks like a list of names and bank accounts. Mentions Preston a few times."

She dropped it into a stunned Sheriff Westbrook's hand.

"Wow. This is a find. No wonder Kingsley was worried about you. Someone told those higher up about putting this in your things." His gaze locked with Liam's. "This needs to go to the FBI. Miller can't find out about it."

"Is he on the take?" Liam frowned.

"I don't know, but he's skipped over some things that lead me to believe he might be."

"You want me and Spencer to take it?"

"No." The sheriff shook his head. "It's too dangerous. The feds can come get it. If you'd stop by the station and tell the two agents who should have arrived yesterday, I'd appreciate it. In the meantime…" he set the drive on the rolling table and turned the bedpan upside down over it.

Liam laughed. "Not much of a safe. I'll let you know once we've notified the feds."

"Appreciate it. Having it here puts a big target on me."

"Let's finish the thumb drive business before we eat," Liam said as they climbed back in his truck.

"Sounds good to me."

The man and woman from the FBI had arrived on schedule. Liam told them behind closed doors about the thumb drive.

"We'll head over there right now," the man said. "This could be just what the department needs in order to put Preston away for a very long time."

With the thumb drive completely out of their hands, a weight lifted from Liam's shoulders. Unless…he turned to Alisa in the truck. "Did you make a copy of that drive?"

Her eyes widened. "What makes you think that?"

"Not an answer." He gritted his teeth.

"Yes." She hitched her chin. "We might need something to bargain with at some point. No one will know."

"Just when I thought our part in this was over." He exhaled heavily and drove to the diner.

Inside, he ordered a four-egg meat and cheese omelet. Alisa ordered biscuits and gravy.

"Are you angry?" She unwrapped her straw and stuck it in her glass of water.

"No, I would've liked to be consulted. This doesn't affect only you anymore. You're living in my house, on my property."

She scowled. "I can move out."

"Don't be ridiculous." He lowered his voice so they wouldn't attract attention, knowing what kind of a gossip mill the diner could be. "I like you right where you are."

"Then what's the problem?" She took a drink of her water, her lips around the straw reminding him of their kiss.

He jerked his gaze away. "I don't want anything to happen to you."

She reached across the table and put her hand on his. "Nobody will know. I just want to go over what's there a little closer. See if we can find out more to tell the sheriff."

After several seconds of frowning at her, he gave up. "We aren't detectives but fine."

"See? I knew you'd see reason."

No, he didn't. Liam saw more danger coming their way. But, she was right. No one would know she'd made a copy. He sure wouldn't tell anyone.

They rushed through breakfast before picking up Spence. When his wife saw Alisa, she wanted to come along.

"This isn't a shopping excursion," Spence said. "We're on official business."

"We'll sit in the backseat and not be a bother at all." Sierra motioned her head, signaling for Alisa to join her.

"I didn't think you'd mind." Liam gave a sheepish grin. "We're only knocking on doors."

"What if we find Jones? What if he starts shooting?"

"We have guns," the women said in unison.

Liam's blood chilled. "No gunfights, ladies. I mean it. Maybe we shouldn't take them."

"Fine. Come on, Alisa. We'll stay here and get to know each other better." Sierra leaned in the window. "You guys will be boring anyway. The possibility of finding Jones was the only sparkle in a dull day."

Liam wanted to kiss Alisa goodbye as Spence did his wife but wasn't ready to let the world know he'd fallen for the woman. After years of mothers in Misty

Hollow trying to fix him up with their daughters, they'd finally left him alone, believing his story that he intended to live his life as a bachelor. Then, a pretty little thing knocks on his door early one morning and changes all that.

As they drove toward the lake and rental cabins, Liam told his friend about the thumb drive, leaving out that Alisa had copied the files. "It's only a matter of time now. They'll have Preston in prison and his riff-raff run out of Misty Hollow."

"That'll be a day to celebrate. Do we know which cabins belong to the Jones family? Who's running them anyway? Jones?"

"I guess he is. We'll have to ask around. Someone will know which are his cabins. There's bound to be someone living on the grounds to maintain the place."

"Let's assume he's here and be ready for anything."

Liam agreed one hundred percent. The last thing he wanted was to almost be killed again.

Chapter Sixteen

Freddy was bored out of his mind! The grapevine said that Kingsley had skipped town. He dialed Preston.

"You aren't supposed to call this number." The man's voice deepened to a growl. "This isn't my burner phone."

"With Kingsley hiding, I need to know what to do next. I can't keep sitting around here picking my nose."

"You'll do what you're told. The time isn't right for the final showdown. We don't know for sure that Miss Gosling has the thumb drive. If you're so bored, why not be a tick in their sides? Keep them focused on anything but digging up dirt on me." The line went dead.

One thing Freddy really hated was being hung up on—he didn't care who it was. He rubbed his hands together. What could he do to create havoc? And how could he do it without being caught? Might be a little easier with the sheriff out of the way, but O'Ryan, limping or not, was a force to be reckoned with. Freddy would have to be very cautious. He called Avery. "When will everyone be gone from the ranch at the same time?"

"Never. If you want on without being seen, your best chance is when we're all sleeping. Look, dude. I don't want to be involved. The boss is already suspicious. Leave me out of all this." He hung up on Freddy.

People were treating him as if he was a nobody. He wouldn't tolerate that. Maybe the whole town of Misty Hollow needed to pay for the way he'd been treated. But first, the Leaning O Ranch.

~

Alisa set a huge bowl of chicken and dumplings in the middle of the supper table, then rang the bell to call in the men. With Liam no longer using a crutch, he insisted on being out and about even if it meant moving slower.

She stepped onto the back deck. A hot breeze blew. The once green grass in the corral was turning brown from lack of rain.

In the distance, she made out the form of Liam and Buddy making their way to the house. The other men came from different directions. Knowing they'd soon be inside, she set the rest of the table.

She shouldn't be upset about losing Kingsley as a client. The man was dangerous and a crook, but she'd miss the money. His payment had helped her move closer to the goal of owning her own home. Well, she'd have to find more clients. How sad that she'd willingly clean a crook's home because it was good money.

"What's wrong?" Liam asked, entering the house.

How did he always know when something bothered her? Was she really that transparent? "Tired, I guess." Not exactly a lie. She was tired of the whole situation. All she wanted was a peaceful life and time to explore her growing feelings for Liam. "I'll probably go to bed early and read."

From the expression on his face, she didn't think he believed her. She forced a smile and took her seat.

He began asking questions when they did the dishes together. "Ready to talk?"

Alisa sighed. Liam was nothing if not persistent. "It's dumb."

"Nothing about you is dumb." With a soapy finger, he tilted her face up.

"Fine." She resumed drying dishes. "I really liked the money I earned from cleaning Kingsley's house. I'll miss it."

His eyes widened for a minute, then he burst into laughter. When he sobered, he asked, "Are you in a financial hardship? Because, I can pay you to clean this place."

"You already are in lieu of rent. No, I'm not hard up. I just have a goal I'm working toward, and it'll go slower now."

"Mind sharing?" He drained the water from the sink.

"I want to own my own house someday."

"You will. See you in the morning. I've some paperwork to do." He tapped her nose and headed to his downstairs office.

After the dishes were dried and put away, Alisa put on the yoga pants and tank top she slept in and settled against propped-up pillows to read. She wasn't sure how long she dozed off before opening her eyes. Alisa blinked several times before realizing the orange glow from her bedroom window wasn't a figment of her imagination. She climbed from bed and glanced out, expecting to see the sunrise. Not even close.

Flames licked the base of the barn. Frightened

neighs rang from the horses.

Oh, Lord.

Alisa slipped her feet into flip-flops then raced to Liam's room and pounded on the door. "Barn's on fire!"

The door flung open. Liam put on a shirt as he led the way down the stairs. "Ring the kitchen bell long and hard until the men are up, then call the fire department. I have to get the horses out."

Alisa rang the bell until she thought her arm would fall off. With her other hand, she dialed 911 and explained the situation. Despite the request not to hang up, she did and sprinted for the barn. Liam wouldn't be able to handle the horses by himself.

"Keep the fire from spreading," he told the ranch hands. "Willy, you help with the horses."

"I'll help, too." Alisa hitched her chin, showing him she didn't want any argument.

He sighed. "Cover the horse's eyes with a burlap sack. It'll make them easier to handle. Stay away from their hooves. Slip a rope over their neck and move fast."

Nodding, she grabbed a sack from a pile near the door and entered the first stall where Sadie snorted and paced. "Come on, girl. Let's take you out of here."

The mare's eyes widened, but she allowed Alisa to slip the rope around her neck and blindfold her. She followed her obediently outside. After releasing her in the corral, Alisa headed to the barn for another as Liam and Willy both exited with frightened horses in tow.

The next horse didn't cooperate as well as Sadie. It kept rearing, keeping Alisa from getting close.

"Come on, sweetie." Alisa coughed, smoke burning her eyes. "We can't stay here." She took a step forward.

The horse turned, its side slamming Alisa into the

stall wall. She slid to the straw, the breath knocked from her lungs.

A flame teased at the edge of the floor, promising to fully break through. Alisa struggled painfully to her feet and tried to grab the rope around the horse's neck. Success. Except the horse was more frightened and starting to slam against the stall.

He jerked his head upward. The rope ripped from her hands, cutting into her skin. She hissed against the pain but reached for the rope one more time.

Alisa coughed again and called for help. The smoke blinded her. The heat grew intense. She stumbled from the stall toward where she hoped the door was. "Liam!"

~

Liam turned toward the barn. When Alisa cried out again, he handed the horse's rope to Wyatt and raced back. "Where are you?" He tied a bandana from his pocket over his nose and mouth. It didn't help the tears streaming down his face from the smoke.

"Here."

Somewhere in the center of the barn. He leaned over, trying to stay under the smoke, to where Alisa blindly held her hands out.

"I couldn't get Storm out of his stall."

"Let's get you out." He spotted Willy climbing high enough to drop the sack over the horse's head. "Willy has Storm." He put his hand around her waist and led her to the back door.

He shoved against it to open it. The door didn't budge. They'd have to find their way back out the front or…he tried to find something to use to break down the door. It wouldn't be easy. His father had built the barn to withstand everything except a fire.

"How are we going to get out?" Alisa's frightened question barely rose above the sound of the crackling flames.

"I'll find a way." He coughed and tried to stifle the next one. It didn't work.

A banging came from the other side. Then, a splintering. Someone tried to break them out.

Liam pulled Alisa to the floor, doing his best to keep them down where the smoke wasn't as thick. He couldn't do anything about the searing heat.

A minute later, Willy opened the door and dragged them into the fresh air and a safe distance from the burning barn. "Someone nailed a board over the door. This fire was no accident. Wasn't any of the ranch hands. They've been in the bunkhouse all night. I know that, because I wasn't sleeping well."

"Thanks for thinking of the back door." Liam wobbled to his feet and helped Alisa to hers. "Fire department here yet?" He spewed another round of wracking coughs, Alisa's coughs joining in. They could both do with some oxygen.

Instead, they'd have to make do with standing upwind. "Fire anywhere else?"

"Started spreading to the pasture, but the boys dug a trench and started dumping buckets of water on the flames. Held it back. For now. We might want to wet the horse blankets in the supply room. If one spark hits the grass…"

"Do it." The blankets had never been used, meant to replace the old ones now burning in the barn. At this point all he could do was pray insurance would cover the cost of all that was going up in smoke. At least no lives were lost, not a single person or animal.

Buddy streaked past him, hackles raised, barking as if he wanted those living in the next county to hear him. Something was up. Liam wanted to follow the dog, but until the fire was out, he couldn't leave.

He turned on the water at the back of the house and started hosing down the wood siding.

"I'll do that to the—" The wailing of sirens cut off her words. The firetruck had arrived. Within seconds the place swarmed with firemen, and Liam and Alisa sat on the edge of the ambulance with oxygen masks in place.

Alisa mumbled something.

Liam frowned and pointed to his ear.

She pulled the mask away from her face. "Why did it take the firemen so long to arrive?"

"They're thirty minutes away." He set the mask aside, most of the stinging in his throat and lungs dissipated. "Out here, we have to make do until help arrives." He glanced to where Buddy had disappeared and not returned. "I need to go look for my dog."

"I'll come with you." She hopped from the ambulance. "Let me get my gun and a flashlight."

Both good ideas. Liam did the same and met up with her on the back deck.

Confident that Willy could handle things at the house, Liam led the way across the pasture and into the dark woods. He'd think about the loss of his barn later. Something had lured Buddy in here, and the dog hadn't returned.

Alisa slipped her hand in his. "We'll find him," she whispered.

Her touch soothed some of the fear. Buddy often stayed gone for a while, chasing after one thing or another. What was different this time was the fact he'd run off with aggression.

Tracking during a dry spell wasn't easy. The packed ground didn't lend itself to footprints left behind. He swung the flashlight's beam from right to left and back again, sweeping the foliage on each side of the game trail. Buddy's dark fur wouldn't help them in the dark.

A whimper came from the right. Liam crashed through the brush, Alisa on his heels.

Buddy lay under a bush, a small puddle of blood next to him. A scrap of denim lay next to the blood.

"Come on, boy. Where are you hurt?" Buddy had just been released by the vet from the accident. The dog limped out, holding his right leg up. He bled from a small gash on his upper leg. A knife?

Liam petted his dog and studied the ground. "Looks like Buddy got into a scuffle with someone and left his mark. Whoever set fire to my barn now has my dog's teeth imprint in his flesh."

"Good. I hope it festers." Alisa's mouth twisted.

"Me, too." Liam scooped Buddy into his arms and headed home. He hoped the culprit died of gangrene.

Chapter Seventeen

Stupid dog. Freddy wished he'd slit its throat instead of a mild jab. He needed a gun.

Back at his house, he poured vodka into the wounds, almost biting off his tongue as his leg screamed. Then, he wrapped it with a clean dish towel. There was no time to sit and cry. He had havoc to create.

Freddy limped to the shed out back and gathered the last two gas cans and some oily rags. There wasn't as much accelerant as he'd like, but it would do. He drove slowly down Main Street, smiling when he noticed O'Ryan's truck outside the veterinary office. Might as well be his first stop.

~

The vet cleaned Buddy's wound. "He'll need a few stitches but won't be down for long. This fella needs to take things a bit slower. First the car accident, now this." He shot Liam a sharp look as if implying he didn't take care of his dog.

"He took off after someone he considered a threat. This didn't happen at home."

"Hmmph." The vet gathered his supplies.

"He's telling the truth." Alisa wiped her bleeding hand on her pants. She'd take care of the rope burn later.

"Let me see your hand while the painkiller takes effect on Buddy." The vet held out his hand.

"It's fine."

"Might as well let him look at it," Liam said. "If you'd stayed home and cleaned it, you wouldn't need him to."

All she could think about was Buddy. She held out her hand. "We had a fire. A frightened horse ripped the rope from my hand." Alisa bit her lip as the vet poured antiseptic across her palm.

"It's deep but won't require stitches. You clean houses, right?"

Alisa nodded.

"Make sure you wear a glove on this hand. You won't want to get any cleaning liquid on it until it's fully healed." He wrapped her hand and turned to Buddy, dismissing the other humans in the room.

Alisa shot Liam an amused look. The vet appeared to favor animals over people.

Liam's phone rang, and he stepped back a few feet to answer it. After a couple of minutes, he slid his phone back in his pocket. "That was Willy. Said Miller showed up, took their statements, and said he'd meet us here to take ours."

"I doubt we can tell him anything more than the others did, but okay." She lowered onto a chair in the corner.

The vet finished the last stitch, then scratched behind Buddy's ears. "Keep him on a leash for a while. He isn't a puppy anymore and needs time to recuperate." He pulled a leash off the wall and handed it to Liam. "You can bring this back next time you're in town."

Alisa sniffed. Was that smoke? She rushed to the

door and opened it. Tendrils of smoke curled under a door opposite them. "Fire."

"What?" the men said in unison.

"The place is on fire."

"The animals." The vet raced from the room and down the hall, turning left past the fire.

Alisa followed.

Liam called out, "I'll join you as soon as I have Buddy safely in the truck."

She waved a hand and followed the vet into a large roomful of about ten caged dogs and cats. "Do you have any boarded in another room?"

"No." He unclipped two cages and grabbed one in each hand. "The door opposite us leads outside. Some of these animals are recuperating from surgery. Be as gentle as you can while moving fast."

At least they'd be easier than a spooked horse. Alisa grabbed two cages containing cats and followed him outside, ignoring the pain in her palm. There were more important things at stake than a dull throbbing. Saving the animals.

Sirens sounded outside. Hopefully, they'd arrived in time to prevent the clinic from being a total loss like Liam's barn.

She set the cages down next to the other ones and returned inside to grab more cages.

"I'll bring them out." Liam put a hand on her shoulder. "Rest your hand. Wait for the firemen and show them where the fire started. I don't want you in danger again."

She nodded and headed around the front of the building. Already flames shot over the clinic's roof. Firemen poured from the fire truck. Alisa pointed to the left side of the building and turned to greet Miller.

"Quite a coincidence, don't you think?"

If he gritted his teeth any harder, they'd break. "I'll bet my favorite sandwich we'll find accelerant, just like at the ranch."

"You think an arsonist is following us?" She tilted her head.

"No. I believe he's trying to keep us from focusing on the drugs and prostitutes." He strode away from her.

Quite an assumption. While Alisa agreed, she also thought the deputy might have inside information. She didn't have a solid reason to suspect him, but since the sheriff didn't trust the deputy, neither would she.

Alisa leaned against the truck, petting Buddy through the open window and waited for Liam while the firemen turned hoses on the flames. "Things are really getting bad, boy." She almost regretted choosing Misty Hollow as her new home.

~

Liam widened his eyes as Miller charged past. "What's up?"

"Another fire. The hardware store this time. That place will go up like an inferno."

"Need help?"

"You are deputized." He slid in his car, shouting at the fire chief to send some of the men to the other fire, then sped away.

"Come on. I've been called to help." Liam motioned for Alisa to hurry to the truck. "Or do you want me to call Willy to come for you?"

"I'm fine staying with you." Exhaustion etched across her face.

He could sympathize. It had been a long, tiring

night, and dawn wasn't coming for a couple more hours. What they needed was a long, uninterrupted sleep.

When they reached the next fire, Spencer Thorne had already arrived in the volunteer fire truck and was dousing flames. "Hey, Liam. Grab another hose. I need help. Don the protective gear, too."

"Will you stay in the car?" He glanced at Alisa.

"Yes. Buddy and I will be right here. I'm going to sit in the backseat with him."

Liam smiled, guessing they'd both be asleep by the time he finished. He hurried to the other truck and donned the gear, then unrolled the other hose and aimed it at the fire. Who was trying to burn down Misty Hollow? If whoever it was set another one, there'd be no one to fight it. All the city had were two fire trucks and one was driven by volunteers.

"Where's the other volunteers?" He yelled over the crackling of the flames.

"On their way," Spence said. "I think it's going to be a loss, though. We all live up on the mountain. Couldn't get here in time."

Miller cursed behind them. "The bank's on fire. I'm going to strangle this arson."

Liam glanced back. "Stay here or go?"

"Stay. The fire is out at the vet clinic. They'll head to the bank. Hopefully in time." The big man bustled back to his car.

Liam almost felt sorry for him. With the sheriff down, and the loaned officers busy with the crime spree, the overweight deputy had too much on his shoulders.

The other volunteers arrived soon. With their help, the fire didn't spread to the diner, but the shop, full of oil and gas, didn't survive. The building lay in smoldering ruins, much like Liam's barn. He shot out a deep breath and removed his helmet.

"Go on home," Spence told him. "I heard about your barn. You've done enough tonight. The rest of us can stay until there's no more threat of the fire starting back up."

"You sure?" It sounded wonderful to Liam.

"Yeah. Go."

He didn't have to be told again. He stripped out of the gear and returned to the truck where Alisa lay curled up on the backseat with Buddy.

The dog wagged his tail without lifting his head.

"Enjoy, Bud." Liam wished it was him instead of his four-legged friend. Curling up with Alisa sounded wonderful.

When they arrived at the ranch, the horses neighed from the corral. No lights burned in the bunkhouse.

Liam opened the back door on his truck. "Come on, sweetheart. I can't carry both of you." He scooped Buddy into his arms.

"I'm coming." She groaned and climbed out of the truck.

"I'll follow you."

Nodding, she trudged to the house, then headed straight to the sofa.

Liam smiled, laying Buddy on his dog bed in the corner. He might get his chance to cuddle after all.

Once he'd made sure the dog was comfortable, he settled on the sofa, reclining a bit. Something poked him. He squeezed his hand behind him and pulled the gun from his waistband he'd forgotten about. As comfortable as he could get, he pulled Alisa against the curve of his shoulder. She murmured something in her sleep. Liam's smile widened right before he closed his eyes.

He jerked awake when the front door opened. How could he have forgotten to lock the door?

Willy shoved Avery inside. "He has something to tell you."

Liam helped a groggy Alisa sit up. "Talk."

Avery squared his shoulders. "I know who is setting the fires. Well, I didn't see him, but I think it's Freddy Jones."

"Why do you say that?" It didn't surprise Liam. The man had been his first guess, too.

"Freddy called yesterday and wanted to know if there'd be a time no one would be on the ranch." He cleared his throat. "I told him I wanted no part of it, but if he didn't want to be seen, he should do it at night. I had no idea he intended to burn the place down."

Liam's neck heated. "What did you think he wanted to do?"

"Leave a message."

"Looks like he did." Liam rubbed his hands briskly down his face.

"You going to fire me?"

"I ought to, but no." He stood. "You coming to me about Freddy shows you aren't full of evil intent toward me. I do need to know if you see him again."

"I swear. We've been friends since high school, but this is not good what he's doing."

Liam nodded and reached for his phone to call the sheriff. When the other man answered, he asked, "You hear about all the fires?"

"Yep. Sorry about your barn."

"My ranch hand, Lars Avery, said it's Freddy Jones setting the fires. Based on a conversation they had but not by seeing it done."

"Once we locate the man, I'll send Miller and one of the other officers to bring him in. All we have right now is circumstantial, same as we had with Kingsley until he shot me."

"My dog took a bite out of whoever did burn my barn. We can always compare his bite to any puncture wounds. Spence and I are headed into Langley tomorrow to search for Jones. No sign of him on the mountain or around Misty Hollow."

"Be careful. You know what he's capable of."

Chapter Eighteen

Although reluctant, Liam left Avery to watch over Alisa and Buddy while he went with Spence to try and locate Jones. Willy and Dane James were busy rounding up a few head of cattle that somehow got loose. He didn't believe that for a second. With all that had happened in Misty Hollow, he'd bet Buddy's favorite ball that the cattle had been let out.

"I'll be fine." Alisa rubbed at the frown mark between his eyes. "I have Buddy, Avery, and my gun, and I can see anyone coming from the road or the woods. Go find Jones."

He leaned his forehead against hers. "Don't do anything I wouldn't want you to do."

She giggled. "You know me so well, but this time I promise to keep my promise."

"That's all I can ask." He gave her a quick kiss as a horn sounded out front, patted Buddy on the head, exchanged a serious look with Avery who entered through the back door, and then rushed to Spence's car.

"Ready to put the man behind bars?" Spence turned the car from the drive and onto the main road that would lead through Misty Hollow and on to Langley.

"Yes." Liam was ready to see where a relationship

with Alisa would go. Getting to know each other was hard enough without danger knocking on his door at regular intervals. He did know that he really cared for her. More than as a friend.

Spence must have been as lost in his thoughts as Liam because they both jumped when Liam's phone rang. "It's the sheriff. Hey, Sheriff. What do you need?"

"Just checking up on you two."

"We're just now entering the Langley city limits. Jones's family owns two properties, so it shouldn't be too long before we know whether he's at one of them. I'll call you as soon as we know something."

The man sighed. "Wish I wasn't laid up. I'm going stir crazy in this house. Good news is I can spend a lot of time on the computer. Found out where Kingsley might be hiding if you can swing by there while you're in Langley. It's a rental he once used." He rattled off an address that Liam committed to memory.

"Will do."

"Heard Miller had you fighting fires."

"Yes, sir. Not enough men for the night we had."

"I don't know what's happening with this town. You two be careful." The sheriff hung up.

"He gave us an address Kingsley might be hiding at." Liam found some paper in the glove compartment and jotted down the address.

"We have all day. That'll be our first stop." Spence slowed the car in front of a red brick house. "Someone's here."

A small silver sedan sat in the carport. "Looks too humble for Kingsley." Liam shoved open his door. "Which might make it the perfect hiding place."

The two strolled to the front door. Liam rang the

doorbell. Not hearing it from inside the house, he rapped sharply.

A heavily made-up woman opened the door. She eyed them up and down. "What do you want?"

"We're looking for a Mr. Kingsley," Liam said.

She gave a flirtatious grin. "Swing that way, do you?"

Liam glanced at Spence, then back at the woman. "I'm not sure I know what you mean."

"Guess you aren't cops, then. This is a house of…entertainment, gentlemen. I run the place. Name is Mildred."

Oh. Liam raised his brows. "Someone told us Kingsley stayed here."

"Sometimes." She crossed her arms, increasing the cleavage over the tight shirt she wore.

"Is he here now?" Spence asked.

"That answer will cost you. I'm in this business to make money, same as my girls. Nothing is for free."

Spence blew air out his nose and pulled his wallet from his pocket. "How much?"

"Fifty from each of you or one of you pays a hundred." Her grin widened.

"Only if you answer another question." Liam scowled. "Know a man named Freddy Jones?"

"One of our regulars." She held out her hand.

"Giving you this money allows us entrance." Spence slapped his money into her hand.

She stepped aside after Liam paid her. "Suit yourself. Leave my girls alone, though. That'll cost more."

As soon as they entered, Mildred gave a piercing whistle.

A bedroom door slammed open, and a half-dressed Kingsley bolted out. He gave a startled glance at Liam and Spence, then darted down the hall.

They gave chase in time to see him race out the back door and scale a fence. No way they'd catch him.

Liam shook his head at the woman hiding under the sheets of the room he stood in. Pretty young thing. Surely, she could find a better job.

Back in the car, he said, "I'll report this place to the sheriff, but they'll pack up and be gone by the time I do." He sent Westbrook a text.

"Yep. Let's see if we have more luck catching Jones."

Liam stared out the window. They'd been so close to grabbing Kingsley.

A young family occupied the next house, and while they paid rent through a management company, they only knew Jones by name. Liam thanked them for their time and joined Spence back in the car.

"Your limp is improving."

Liam closed his door. "No choice with all this running around, fighting fires, and catching bad guys." He laughed. "I can honestly say, though, I'm ready to turn this badge in. I'm a rancher, not a law man."

"I'm ex-military and this is a lot for me, too. But, I've been in trouble before and came out okay. We'll get you and Alisa through this."

He sure hoped so. The bad guys always seemed a step ahead of them.

The last house didn't look occupied. Weeds covered the lawn. Boards covered most of the windows. The place hadn't been lived in for a long time.

"Might as well see if we can find out anything."

Liam shoved his door open as Spence did the same.

Liam headed around back. A board had been removed from a window. He reached for the knob on the back door. It turned under his hand.

Waving at Spence that he was going in, he stepped into a dark kitchen and stood still, his ears straining to hear anything. A scrape sounded from another room. He motioned to Spence and pointed.

Spence nodded and followed.

Footsteps pounded.

Glass shattered.

Liam and Spence sprinted outside after the fleeing Jones who had a towel wrapped around a blood-stained thigh. "Stop!" Liam shouted.

Jones fired a quick shot over his shoulder.

How could the man move so fast with an injured leg? Liam screamed as he sprinted after him.

Spence easily passed him.

Jones fired again. The bullet grazed Spence's arm, slowing him.

Liam took aim, squeezed the trigger and missed.

Jones dashed through a neighboring back door. Screams followed. A few seconds later, he raced down the street behind where they stood.

Liam groaned and headed for the car. "Let's go have your arm looked at."

~

Freddy cursed and headed for Bill's garage. "I need a car."

"I don't want any trouble." Bill shot a worried look at the two goons Preston had sent. "I have too much work to do and no help. All they do is sit around and glare at everyone who comes in."

"Give me a vehicle and there won't be any trouble." Freddy leaned against the wall, his leg killing him. "And a clean coverall. I need to change out of these clothes."

"What happened?"

"Dog bite." O'Ryan and his mutt were going to pay.

Bill tossed him a clean coverup and keys. "The green truck out back. Try not to wreck it. It's my loaner."

"Thanks." Jones headed to the restroom to clean his leg again, then donned the clean clothes.

He'd hit the mountain man but not enough to drop him. Hopefully, it was enough to keep them occupied while he exacted his revenge.

~

Alisa made a simple lunch for herself and Avery of egg salad sandwiches and homemade French fries. She carried her lunch into the living room and settled on the sofa with a book, her plate next to her. Her finger wagged at Buddy when he tried to snag a fry. "No, sir."

The morning had been spent cleaning not only her small house but Liam's large one. There was no way she could be confined to the house the next day. She had work to do. The bookstore had agreed to wait another day, but it wasn't fair to any of her clients. At this rate, she'd be losing them, and Alisa would never have a house of her own. Nothing big or fancy; something small and cute like the house out back.

Alisa bit into her sandwich. Her dream might be changing, though. She really liked waking up under the same roof as Liam. Maybe marriage should be her choice now. A family of her own instead of a house. The idea definitely had merit, especially if Liam was part of that dream.

"I'm going to walk the perimeter," Avery said from the kitchen doorway. "Won't be gone more than a few minutes."

"Okay." Alisa opened her book and immersed herself in a mystery about a dog getting its human into trouble.

The back door opened, the screen banging closed. It hadn't taken Avery long to walk around the house.

Buddy growled, his hackles raised.

Alisa closed her book and slowly rose to her feet. She waved for Buddy to follow and made her way upstairs, placing each foot with caution, stepping over the stairs that creaked. After cleaning the house as many times as she had, she knew every creak.

In her room, she closed the door and locked it before removing her gun from her nightstand. If Liam knew she hadn't kept it with her, he'd be livid.

Gun in hand, she moved to the bathroom, taking a growling Buddy with her and locked that door, too. Whoever snuck into the house would have to go through two locked doors and her gun to get to her.

A step creaked.

She put her hand on Buddy's muzzle to keep him from barking. "Shh." Her heart beat in her throat so hard she feared whoever approached her door would hear.

"Hey!" Avery's voice boomed.

A shot rang out.

A muffled thud.

Alisa clapped one hand over her mouth, the one holding the gun trembling so hard she doubted she could hit anything. Please, God.

What if he set fire to the house? She'd be trapped.

But if he planned to do that, then why come inside? No one was home except for her and Avery who might now be dying at the foot of the stairs.

Someone pounded against the bedroom door. It banged open.

Alisa clutched the gun with both hands and tried to still her shaking.

Buddy's barks echoed in the tiled room and made her ears ache. He dug at the door.

"Get back," she hissed, her eyes wide. The door would slam open any minute. She'd only have one chance to fire.

The banging started.

Tears choked her. "Go away. I have a gun, and I will shoot." She fired through the door.

The banging stopped.

"Alisa!" Liam called from downstairs.

"Go back." Oh, please go back. "He has a gun." She fired again.

Pounding footsteps retreated. Another gun shot.

Alisa gasped. Not Liam, too.

Buddy whimpered, his scratching at the door growing in intensity.

More footsteps returning.

She held her breath.

"It's me."

She scrambled for the door, unlocking it, then threw herself into Liam's arms. "When I heard the shot…how's Avery?" She peered into the face she loved.

"He's lost a lot of blood, but I don't think he'll die." He cupped her face. "It was Jones. He got away. Spencer Thorne is giving chase, but I doubt he'll catch him. Tell me you're okay." He pulled her close.

"Other than frightened, I'm fine. I wasn't going to make it easy for him."

His chest rumbled with laughter. "That's my girl."

She smiled. "Am I your girl?"

"The one and only."

"Everyone okay up there?" Spencer called out.

"Yes. We're coming down." Liam took Alisa's hand. "Come on, Buddy. You did a good job today."

They joined Spencer downstairs. "He vanished," he said. "This isn't the last time we'll see Jones. Liam, you need to hire some extra men out here. You can't have just one on the ranch."

Liam agreed. Their safety was more important than money.

Chapter Nineteen

Freddy called the sheriff's department and asked for Miller. "You have to help me, man. My leg ain't doing so good. I think it's infected." He lay a hand over his throbbing, warm thigh. Did he have a fever? His face felt hot. No wonder he felt like hell.

"If you'd lay low for a while, you wouldn't be feeling this way. Where are you?"

"In that shed back of Bill's place. You coming to pick me up?"

"Yes, but I need to pick up Kingsley first. The two of you are going to give me a heart attack. After this, I want both of you out of Misty Hollow for good. I'll bring some antibiotics." He hung up.

Freddy wasn't leaving until O'Ryan was six feet under. When he was fired, he lost everything. No money, no woman, no consistent place to live. Who wanted a cowboy without a ranch? Sure, he made some money from his family's rental properties, but after paying the bills there wasn't much left. He'd make O'Ryan pay with cash, then with his life. He'd shoot that dog, too. Then, when revenge was paid, he'd ask Preston if he could move up the ranks to Kingsley's spot. The only sand in that biscuit was the fact Freddy didn't have a business to launder money through. Freddy couldn't think straight with his head and leg throbbing. He groaned and rested his head against the rough cement wall behind him.

He must have fallen asleep because he opened his eyes to Miller kicking his foot. "Stop it."

"You look bad." He held out a bottle of pills. "Bought these on my trip to Mexico."

"Thanks." He swallowed two of them dry.

"Let's go. Kingsley is in the car. Bill won't be happy to find you here."

He didn't care what made Bill happy. It had started to rain, and the building kept him dry. Freddy struggled to his feet and limped to the car. He'd have to steal a crutch from somewhere. Every step he took sent fire through his leg. "Where are we going?" he asked after sliding into the back seat of the squad car. He shuddered, hating the back seat of any law enforcement vehicle.

"There's a cabin a few miles down Misty creek. The two of you can hole up there until Preston needs you. I've stocked it with food and water, sleeping bags—everything you need." Miller glanced in the rearview mirror.

"Good." Freddy leaned against the door and closed his eyes. He really needed some rest.

He woke again when the car stopped in front of a cabin. "I should've driven myself." Freddy bit his tongue to keep from whimpering as he struggled out of the car. "I don't have a way of getting around now."

"You won't need one. Turn around."

Freddy tensed. The plan all along was for them to get rid of him. He pulled his gun from the waistband of his pants and whipped around. His shot took Kingsley in the chest. The other man's shot pinged the side of the car. Freddy fired through the windshield, disposing of Miller.

Who's the loser here, guys? His shoulders slumped. He could dump Kingsley anywhere, but the deputy would have to be driven somewhere, then Freddy would have to walk back. This was not his day.

After dragging the not yet, but very soon-to-be dead Kingsley into the woods, Freddy shoved Miller's body aside and climbed into the driver's seat and did his best to ignore the fact the other man's blood covered the seat and steering wheel.

He drove to Misty Lake. A few minutes later, he watched as the car went rear end up into the water. It sank halfway before getting hung up on something. A big rock most likely. Freddy didn't care. He'd be in hiding before Miller's body was discovered.

~

"Need to see you at the office." Liam read a text from the sheriff. The office? The man hadn't been released to go back to work, had he?

Alisa had gone to clean houses despite Liam's protests. She'd been smart enough to wait until he was busy in the barn before sneaking out. He sent her a text as to where he'd be and asked her not to return to the ranch until he could be there.

When she replied back that she'd wait for him at the diner, he made sure Buddy was comfortable, then drove to the sheriff's office without worrying about Alisa. He arrived at the same time as Spencer. "Know what's going on?"

"Not yet, but I have a feeling the sheriff is back." He grinned and held the door open for Liam.

Sheriff Westbrook sat in the conference room. From the lines on his face, it wasn't hard to guess the man shouldn't be here.

"What's so important that you had to get out of bed?" Liam nodded at the two suits in the room. He hadn't met the feds yet, but these two looked as if they'd been carved from the same stone right down to the dark hair and eyes.

"These are Special Agents Beck and Winter." He stood. "We're headed to Misty Lake where a couple of police officers say a car that looks like one of ours is half-sunk."

Back straight and stony-faced, the sheriff led the way to his car out front. Parked next to it was a black SUV.

Twenty minutes later, sirens blaring and lights flashing, they arrived at the lake. Sure enough, the back end of a squad car reached for the sky. A tow truck idled nearby waiting for orders to pull the car from the water.

Westbrook gave the order.

The truck slowly pulled the car from the lake and left it on the ground rather than prepare it to be towed. Liam followed the sheriff to the front.

The windshield had been shattered. "Looks like a bullet hole." He feared the worst.

"Yep, that's what it is." The sheriff moved to the passenger window. "Miller's inside."

No need to check and see whether the man was alive. If he wasn't shot, he'd have drowned.

"I thought he was one of the bad guys." Spence stood off to the side, arms crossed.

"They aren't remiss about killing their own." The sheriff called for an ambulance. "This is why I'm back to work. After receiving the call, I had no choice. Someone has to run this circus." He jerked his head to the two feds who now circled Miller's car. "The investigation is officially theirs, but they do need local backup. That's us."

How could he keep Alisa safe if he had to remain a full-time deputy? Liam strolled to the water's edge. He couldn't leave the sheriff short-handed, especially since he wasn't fully healed yet. Spence and the two borrowed officers would be stretched thin even with the feds. But working would leave Alisa on the ranch without him.

His men could handle the livestock, but could they do their jobs and play bodyguard?

"You can hand your badge back." The sheriff stepped to his side. "You're only a volunteer. I know Miss Gosling needs you."

"So does this town." The sun sparkled on the lake's surface. Liam squinted against the glare. "I've lived here my whole life. Can't just turn my back on my town."

"You can't jeopardize the life of the woman you love either. Believe me, I've been there." He held out his hand. "Hand it over. I understand."

"What about your reasons for giving it to me in the first place? That danger still exists."

"Then I'm assigning you guard duty." He gave a sad smile. "I'm assigning you to watch over Miss Gosling like you did before you were back on two legs. Saves me having to send another officer to shadow her. If I absolutely need you, I'll give you a call."

"Thank you. You can drop me at the diner when we're done here."

~

"Seems like every year something bad happens in this town." Wilbur, as usual, sat at the counter and complained about the city he said he'd never move from. "Serial killers, stalkers, organized crime, arson, I can't think of what this city hasn't had happen."

"Those things are everywhere," someone else said. "Misty Hollow just got lucky for a while. Give it time. Peace will come again. Everything cycles around in time."

"If you live long enough," Wilbur mumbled.

Alisa smiled over her BLT with cream cheese instead of mayo. Living long enough was definitely key, especially with what had happened since she rented that little house.

She glanced around the crowded diner, focusing in on women around her own age. Would she live long enough to set down roots and make friends? Not until Preston and his minions were behind bars. Alisa set her sandwich down. Every day was a gift. Each time she went downstairs and laid eyes on Liam, it was priceless. She didn't want to know life without that. Not anymore. When this was all done, she planned on telling him exactly how much she loved him.

As if she'd conjured him with her thoughts, Liam strolled in. He glanced around and gave a warm smile when he spotted her.

Women's heads turned as he passed them, but he didn't glance to the left or the right. His eyes stayed locked on Alisa.

Her face heated. The way he looked at her made her feel both beautiful and just a little naughty at the thoughts that flickered through her mind.

He slid in the booth across from her, his smile widening. "I have been ordered to be your bodyguard. No more leaving you alone."

"More of following me around as I clean businesses and houses?" She laughed and picked up her sandwich.

"Want a bite?"

"No, I think I'll get my own." He ordered a fully loaded hamburger. "Miller's body was found in his squad car in Misty Lake. Sheriff Westbrook said I could stay with you unless he absolutely needs me."

"That sounds perfect." Twenty-four hours in Liam's company. What could be better? "We can watch the sun rise on the mountain again." Could they get married in that spot overlooking the valley? It seemed the perfect spot to her. She glanced at Liam from under lowered lashes. Would he think so? "Who does the sheriff think killed Miller?" she asked.

"Kingsley? A hit ordered by Preston? Who knows at this point? It could even be Jones." He straightened so the waitress could set down his order. "Maybe we'll be lucky, and they'll kill each other off."

Two men in coveralls who didn't look as if they'd ever been under a vehicle entered the diner. Both shot glances toward the booth Alisa and Liam sat in, then quickly looked away.

Alisa narrowed her eyes. It almost seemed as if they'd come to find her. She gave herself a mental shake. Stop looking for trouble.

Liam stared at the two men.

"Do you know them?" Alisa asked.

"New mechanics at Bill's garage."

"They don't look like mechanics. I bet their fingernails are clean."

"No, they don't look like mechanics."

"Preston's men?" Her heart gave a hitch.

"Yes, and they seemed to be looking for you."

Liam having the same thought as she did made her mouth as a dry as a dead leaf.

Chapter Twenty

Earbuds in her ears, Alisa rode Sadie past the corral where Liam worked with a horse. She sang along with the sea shanty. "Put him in bed with the captain's daughter!" She giggled at the shocked look on Liam's face. She really ought to introduce him to the songs she enjoyed so much. "Way-hay and up she rises…"

After two weeks of no one following them, breaking into the house, or any of the other things that had plagued them and Misty Hollow not so long ago, Liam deemed it safe enough for Alisa to ride again as long as she stayed on the ranch.

She glanced back to see Dane James trailing behind. So, she could ride, but she had to have an escort. Ugh. Solitude was already in short supply on the ranch. As the only woman, Alisa needed her alone time. Recreational alone time.

Liam had wanted to come along but said that working would strengthen his leg. She cast a scowl back at Dane.

The ranch hand shrugged.

It wasn't his fault. The man was only following orders.

She urged Sadie into a trot. Dane did the same.

Alisa went faster. So did the ranch hand. The breeze grabbed her laugh and sent it flying. She slowed as she neared the creek. Since the rains, the water almost reached the top of the bank but wasn't flowing too fast for the swim she wanted to take in the widened area under a bluff. Today might be her only chance for a while. More rain was coming in the next day or two.

Knowing Sadie would stay close, she looped the reins around the saddle horn and let the horse graze. From behind the saddle, she grabbed the extra horse blanket and her book and sat under a maple tree.

The morning sun kissed the water. A squirrel scampered from one tree to the next. The sun coming through the tree branches caressed Alisa's legs. Ah, she'd needed this day.

Thankfully, Dane stopped far enough away that she could pretend to be alone with her book. She opened it and started reading about a serial killer who kidnapped young men. With all that had happened around town, she should have chosen a humorous mystery or a romantic comedy.

She froze as a copperhead slithered a few feet away. The snake paid her no attention and disappeared under a bush. Alisa shuddered. She hated snakes. With a careful glance around her to make sure nothing else disrupted her morning, she returned to her book.

"Whoa!"

She peered around the tree to see Dane struggling to contain his horse. Snapping her book closed, she hurried to see a wide-eyed Sadie ready to bolt.

"What's wrong?" She grabbed the horse's reins.

"Darn horse saw a snake and freaked." Dane finally

settled the horse. "That's what happens when the sun comes out after a rain. The snakes want to warm up. You ready to head back?"

She wasn't, really, but two snakes nearby had her gathering her blanket and climbing on Sadie. Maybe she'd go to the lake. With people regularly hiking the area, snakes would be hiding, right?

Liam met them at the edge of the yard. "You weren't gone long."

"Too many snakes, boss." Dane led his horse and Sadie to the barn.

"I think I'll move to the lake to read my book."

"Why not pack a lunch and I'll come along? I could use a break."

Her heart skipped a beat. "Sure. I'll make us some sandwiches." Somehow, knowing Liam wanted to spend time with her dispelled her need for solitude. What could be better than a few hours by the water with Liam?

When she returned outside, Liam had tied a couple of kayaks onto the back of his truck. "I've never tried that before."

"It's easy. You'll have fun. You do know how to swim, don't you?"

"Yes." Alisa eyed the flotation devices stuck under the stretchy black cord behind the kayak's seat. She could swim, but knowing she'd have protection if she fell out relieved some of her anxiety.

"I should have asked you but thought I'd surprise you instead." He tightened the bungee cord. "Is that all right?"

"Sure. It sounds like fun and it's something new." Alisa placed the basket of food and bottled water in the truck bed. Now that she'd thought about it, excitement rose. She could read later.

Liam flashed her a smile as he climbed in the driver's seat. "I have a confession to make."

"Oh?" She tilted her head.

"I didn't want a Sunday to go by without spending at least part of it with you."

Her face had to be the color of a maple leaf in autumn. "Me either." Her voice sounded breathless. She stared out the passenger side window so she didn't embarrass herself at her lack of coherent replies. One would think being tongue-tied when he said something flirty or romantic would have stopped after a while. She really, really liked him—more than like, if she were honest with herself. Time to act like an adult and not a shy teenager.

At the lake, she helped Liam carry the kayaks to a spot where they could enter the water. "You will get your feet wet," he said.

"That's okay." The water wouldn't hurt her sandals. Alisa watched as he climbed into his kayak, then copied him. Her kayak rocked far more than his. She clutched the sides until the kayak steadied.

"Hold the paddles like this. Dip them into the water like this, then this." He pulled away from her, skimming the top of the water.

It didn't take her long to figure it out, and she soon pulled alongside him. "This is fun." When the kayak glided at a good clip, it felt like flying.

A boat sped past them, sending her rocking again. "Isn't that the two new mechanics?"

~

Liam frowned at the boat moving too fast past them. They obviously didn't know boating courtesy. "It does look like them." First thought was they'd been followed, but Bill's was closed on Sundays. The men could simply be out fishing. Still, he'd keep an eye out anyway.

They kayaked along the bank watching nearby cranes take flight. Alisa had taken to kayaking quickly. A peaceful look graced her pretty face. He'd been right about bringing her along. Her face showed kayaking was just as beneficial for her as curling up with a book.

"Ready to head back and have some lunch? We can come back out on the water afterward."

She nodded. "My stomach is growling."

As they rowed toward a picnic table beside the lake, the same boat sped by, closer this time. Liam held his paddle against Alisa's kayak to steady it. "It's almost as if they're trying to capsize us."

Her eyes widened. "You think so? What would that accomplish?"

"There are snakes in this lake. We could be run over by a boat." Possibly them. "I'm most likely borrowing trouble, though." He motioned for her to go faster. A couple of minutes later, they were onshore, their kayaks pulled from the water.

Alisa set out water, apple slices, and ham and cheese sandwiches. "Thank you for this idea. I had no idea how much fun kayaking could be."

"I'll take you down the Buffalo River sometime. You'll love it, and the scenery is beautiful." Not as beautiful as the woman sitting across from him, but if she enjoyed Misty Lake, she'd love the river.

He stared over the water. The two men sat in their boat in clear view of the table where he and Alisa sat. If they were legitimately fishing, they'd be trolling the lake, not staying in one place for a long period of time unless the fish were biting. Liam had yet to see them pull anything from the water.

"You're worried." Alisa put a hand over his. "Maybe we should head back to the ranch."

"And miss out on more kayaking?"

"I'm thinking more along the lines of missing out on ending up in the lake." She arched a brow.

He hated to cut the day short without being positive the men were watching them, but he wouldn't put Alisa in harm's way. "You're right. We'll finish our lunch and head back. Sorry to cut your relaxation short."

"No, you added to it. Now, I'll immerse myself in my book." She smiled and put the used napkins and paper plates back in the basket. "It's afternoon now anyway."

Every time he spent time with her, it passed like a shooting star. He stood and grabbed the front handle on one of the kayaks while Alisa took the end. As he secured the last strap, he glanced back toward the lake. The boat still bobbed on the gentle waves, two heads turned in his direction.

After climbing in the truck, Liam took one more look back. The boat sped toward the dock, leaving no question in his mind that the two men had been there to keep an eye on him and Alisa.

"Did Westbrook ever tell us what happened with the thumb drive?" She asked. "Surely, they know what's on it by now. Maybe we should study the copy I made. Save it to another drive so we have something to give them if they come."

"*When* they come." There was no if. He started the truck. "That is a very good idea."

At the ranch, Alisa retrieved her laptop and pulled

up the files she'd copied. "No matter how many times I look at this, all I see are names and account numbers."

"That's enough to put a crime boss after you. He wouldn't want the names of those he works with to leak out." He sat next to her and handed her a blank drive. "I'm sure the sheriff is checking out each name on that list before having them all taken to their prospective police stations. The feds will definitely be busy with this."

"I just want this all to be over." She sighed, her shoulders slumping. "I'm tired of looking over my shoulder all the time. Sick of wondering whether I'll be grabbed getting out of my car at the house of a client or taken when I leave their house."

He put his arm around her shoulder and pulled her close. "It will be over. Everything comes to an end."

"I don't want me or you to end along with the danger."

"We won't." He'd do everything in his power to make sure that didn't happen. "Come on. You can read in my office. I have some paperwork to do." He stood, reluctant to release her. "You, too, Buddy."

"Want some coffee?" Alisa pocketed the drive. "Won't take me but a minute. I'll bring it in."

"Sounds good." He headed to his office, Buddy padding along behind him.

When Alisa entered with two coffee cups in hand, she set one on his desk and took the other to an end table next to a large chair. She sat and curled her legs under her as she reached for her book.

Liam's phone buzzed. A text from the sheriff. His blood chilled as if someone had filled him with ice water. "Preston just arrived in town."

Alisa jerked her head up. "What does that mean exactly?"

"That things are about to come to a head." His heart dropped to his knees.

Chapter Twenty-one

Preston eyed the three men in front of him. Bill looked startled, as if a bullet landed in his gut for opening the door. The other two hired goons, simply known as Dick and Harry, merely looked bored with a bit of sheepish thrown in. "So you lost them. At the lake. They were in kayaks. You were in a boat. Did I hear that correctly?"

Dick cleared his throat and nodded. "We tried capsizing them, but they wouldn't flip."

"Why didn't you run over them?" That's why he'd come to this hillbilly town. Because these idiots couldn't do their job. "Where are Jones and Kingsley?" He wanted to strangle Jones for killing the deputy. All that had accomplished was to make the water hotter. They were barely holding their heads high enough not to drown as it was. Without Kingsley moving money through the bank…

"Find them. Meet me at Kingsley's house tonight at eight." Preston growled and marched from the garage to his waiting Jaguar. This town didn't even have a good enough place to spend the night, so he headed for Kingsley's big house outside of town.

Preston spent the rest of the day making phone calls,

checking his accounts, and thinking. If the cleaning woman did have the thumb drive, why wasn't anyone arrested yet? He drummed his fingers on the top of a cherrywood desk. Kingsley did have good taste. In his other hand, he twirled a glass of fine bourbon.

The sheriff of a town this size couldn't be playing games. Even if he had been a fed once, his skills had to have dropped living here. This place already had sucked out his ambition. He'd thought a small town hidden in the mountains would be the perfect setup for his operation. Instead, it had been nothing but a headache. He downed his drink and poured another.

To make matters worse, it started to rain. Preston cursed. What he wouldn't do for a big city without dirt roads. By eight o'clock that night, he'd worked himself into a semi-drunken stupor. Didn't matter. He never lost his wits.

His phone rang. "Preston."

"Jones." His voice sounded raspy.

"You sound bad."

"Dog bite infection. I'm on the mend, though. Heard from Harry that there's a meeting tonight?"

"Yes. Where are you?"

"On my way." Click. He actually had the nerve to hang up on Preston.

That man's days were numbered. As soon as Jones was no longer needed, he'd be disposed of. But as bad as he was, he was the best Preston had. The man seemed crazy enough to do anything.

Jones was the last to arrive, limping into the house at five after eight p.m. With no apologies, he planted his sweating self onto a leather chair that cost more than most people made in a month. Preston almost told him to get up, then remembered he didn't own the place, and the man looked ready to keel over at any moment.

"I've called you men here to formulate a plan to get rid of the rancher and his woman. We've seen no evidence of whether she has the thumb drive or not, and I'm tired of waiting. I want out of this place. Everything out. We'll find another town more willing to accept the money we bring to the table. And I'm open to suggestions."

Jones struggled to his feet and lumbered to the decanter on the sideboard. "The woman likes to go for horseback rides. She stops and reads by the creek. It wouldn't take too much effort to stake the area out and grab her the next time she rides. Make it look like she fell from her horse and hit her head." He downed a shot of bourbon and poured himself another. "I want dibs on O'Ryan and the dog, though." He rubbed his thigh.

"You got it." Preston rubbed his chin and stared at Dick and Harry. "The three of us will take care of the woman…if the two of you think you're up to the task."

They glanced at each other, then nodded. "Sure, boss. A dart to the horse's rump should cause the woman to fall off."

"And then someone finds the dart and knows it isn't an accident." He frowned. "Can't you make a loud noise or something?"

"She's afraid of snakes." Jones made his way slowly back to the chair. "So are horses. Toss one in their path." He shook his head as if they were all idiots. "Do I have to do everything?"

Preston didn't like the man's tone. Who did he think he was? Preston was the boss here, not Jones.

"I don't like snakes," Dick said, his face paling.

Preston sighed. "It doesn't have to be a poisonous one. A rubber snake would probably work. Just make sure it isn't left behind. I want the woman dead and the thumb drive in my hand."

"What if she doesn't have it?" Jones rolled his head on his shoulders. "We ain't seen no evidence that she does. What if she's been innocent this whole time, and we're looking at the wrong person?"

It couldn't be anyone else. "No loose ends. If you see a chance, take it."

~

The next morning, Alisa erased the files from her computer. The feds had the original thumb drive, and she had the copy. That was one thumb drive too many. Now, how could she draw the crooks into the open?

She'd have to be alone. Something she never was even when out riding. But she might be able to give the ranch hands assigned to her the slip. The men paid her as little attention as possible when they followed. She'd caught them sleeping while she read more than once. After they dozed, she'd sneak off. When Preston came for her, she'd hand over the flash drive if he'd agree to leave town and never come back.

It would work. It had to.

One glance at the clock had her jumping to her feet. Alisa had a house to clean before returning to the ranch to fix the men's lunch. She almost left without telling Liam. Oh, she was ready to reclaim her life.

Rain poured outside. She grabbed an umbrella and went in search of Liam.

He looked up from currying a horse. "You have a house?"

"Yes."

"It's fixing to storm." He set the brush on a shelf.

"Still have work to do. I can go alone if…"

"No. I have some time." He smiled and cupped her cheek. "There's always time for you, sweetheart."

She leaned into his touch, breathing deeply of horse, hay, and Liam. Very good scents in her mind. "It's only Mrs. Mayfield. Shouldn't take more than an hour, after partaking of a snack."

"Oh, good. I like her." He put his hand on the small of her back and shared the umbrella to the car.

"She likes you, too." In fact, Alisa would be willing to bet that Mrs. Mayfield would have more than liked him if she were thirty years younger.

As expected, she had tea and cookies ready when they arrived and looked more pleased to see Liam than she did Alisa. "You're not limping as much, young man. You'll be in dancing condition real soon."

"There's no dancing around here, Mrs. Mayfield." He planted a tender kiss on her wrinkled cheek.

"We could make our own music." She giggled and led them to the table. "Sit. Have a snack. You aren't in a hurry, are you?"

"As long as I return in time to have lunch ready at noon." Alisa grabbed a cookie. Oatmeal with chocolate chips still warm from the oven.

"My grandson, Dane, told me he's been having to escort you when you go out riding." Mrs. Mayfield's sharp gaze fell on her. "You in some kind of trouble?"

Alisa sent a wide-eyed look Liam's way. He shook his head, then said, "With all the rain we've had, there's been a lot of snakes coming out when the sun shines. We don't want Alisa left out there if her horse spooks."

"That makes sense."

Alisa relaxed. The last thing she wanted or needed was for the folks of Misty Hollow to find out she'd brought trouble to their town. Sure, it might have come anyway, but she was partially at fault if not totally.

She still hoped for the opportunity to settle down, make friends, and call Misty Hollow her home. That wouldn't happen if the townsfolk were mad at her. They'd most likely run her out.

"Did you hear the bank manager has disappeared?" Mrs. Mayfield clicked her tongue. "Vanished without a trace. They did find his car on the side of the road up the mountain. Speculation is—he went for a hike, got lost, and never came out." She brushed cookie crumbs from her bosom. "I think someone killed him because he wasn't exactly an outstanding citizen. There's talk around town that he works for the mob."

How close to the truth she was.

~

"Mrs. Mayfield, you shouldn't go around spreading this kind of news." Liam crossed his arms. "You might draw interest from the wrong type of people."

"You're a real sweetheart, Liam, but I'm not afraid. Besides, I never leave this house. I even have my groceries delivered. It's the delivery guy who fills me in on the local gossip. That and the phone. My friends call on a regular basis to check on me."

"Just be careful." The sound of the vacuum came from the other room. "Is there any work you need done around here? Now that I'm off the crutches, I can do repairs for you."

"A visit is all I need." She took another cookie, then pushed the plate toward him. "Take the last two. You plan on having a relationship with that girl?" She jerked her head in the direction of the vacuum's roar.

"Yes." He grinned.

"What's taking you so long?"

He couldn't tell her they waited until the danger to them was past. The old woman would say, 'why wait when tomorrow might never come?' She'd be right, but once he told Alisa exactly how he felt about her, he'd become distracted. Especially if she didn't share his feelings. No, it was best to wait.

"Do you know why our girl works so hard?" She arched a brow. "Alisa wants to own her own home. Without Kingsley needing her services, that slows down her achieving that dream."

"Why are you telling me this?"

She grinned, her eyes almost disappearing in the folds of her cheeks. "If you asked her to marry you, she wouldn't need to worry about buying a house."

Marriage? He supposed that was the likely step in sealing their relationship. He eyed Alisa through the doorway.

She gathered her supplies and smiled his way.

Yes, he could see himself married to her. They kind of were, without the physical aspect, anyway. Living under the same roof. Seeing her first thing in the morning and last thing at night. The thought of her not being there tore at his heart.

"I can see the thoughts clear on your face. Tell her you love her, Liam. Before it's too late."

Her foreboding words cast a shadow over the day that had nothing to do with the storm clouds overhead. He could miss out on the best thing in his life whether he waited or not. Either they'd survive the danger hanging over them and see how a relationship went, or they'd be killed.

He took Alisa's supplies from her and headed for her car. Across the street stood the same two men who had tried to turn over the kayaks. Liam squared his shoulders and returned the stare. He would not be intimidated. This was his town. No, he wouldn't hide from a couple of two-bit gangsters.

One of them pantomimed making a gun with his fingers, aimed at Liam, and laughed. Then, the two headed toward the diner.

"They're following us." Alisa stepped to his side.

"It appears that way."

"Waiting to grab us?"

"Maybe. Or shoot us when there aren't any witnesses." He motioned to where Mrs. Mayfield stood on her front porch. "I don't think it'll be good for us if they catch us away from people."

"Let's go back to the ranch, then. There's always a hand around."

True, but the three hands were stretched thin as it was. Sometimes, they weren't close enough to the main house to be of any help.

Chapter Twenty-two

The rain and thunder finally stopped. Alisa raced to the barn to saddle Sadie. To her way of thinking, not many things could compare to a horse ride after a rain. The clean air, the smell of damp dirt. She smiled and hefted the saddle onto the horse's back.

"Headed to the creek?" Liam leaned against the barn wall just inside the door.

"Yes. Only for a little while. An hour at the most."

"I'll have Avery follow along behind you."

Knowing it was useless to argue, she nodded. "I'm not even taking a lunch."

"If I weren't so busy, I'd go with you. I love riding right after a rain." He pushed away from the wall. "Be careful. The trail will be slick, and the creek is running swift and high." Liam leaned down and kissed her, his lips and eyes making promises she hoped he could keep. He raised his head and leaned his forehead against hers. "I'll be watching the clock."

"What has you so busy today?"

"The sheriff wants me to go over the thumb drive a little deeper. He seems to think there might be a name of someone who once lived in Misty Hollow. Seems to think I'd know them if I looked hard enough." Liam shrugged. "It's a long shot, but he's almost ready to haul

Preston and his goons in.”

“Good.” Life would return to some semblance of normalcy. She swung onto the saddle. “Tell Avery where I’ve gone. I’m sure he can catch up.”

“Will do.” He gave Sadie a slap on the rump.

As soon as Alisa passed the corral, Avery turned from heading across the fields toward her. She tossed him a wave and continued. Liam had chosen his hands well. They did what he asked without question, even if it was something they’d rather not do. Like babysit her.

She glanced at the gray sky, hoping it wouldn’t rain again until she returned home. The weatherman had said the rain would stop by noon, but the heavy clouds gathering said otherwise.

Despite the threat that might drop on her head, she rode at a leisurely pace. She’d overhead Mrs. Mayfield the day before telling Liam not to let her get away. The timing of one song ending on her earbuds and another beginning had been perfect.

What would he do after talking to the old lady? What would Alisa say if he did ask her to marry him? They’d never dated, only lived in separate rooms under the same roof. Their focus had been on the imminent danger since the first moment they met. Could a relationship formed on that foundation flourish?

She heard the rushing waters of the creek before spotting them. The recent rains had swollen its banks. No peaceful flowing now. A bit of vertigo overtook her as she stared at the rapidly moving water. When she tore her gaze away, the ground seemed to be moving along with the creek.

She spotted Avery a few yards away, sitting on his horse and staring into the distance.

A shot rang out.

He fell from his horse.

Sadie reared.

Alisa slid from the saddle, hit the ground, and rolled into the creek.

As the water swept her away, she frantically grabbed at every low-hanging branch, only to have it torn from her hands. She submerged in the cold water, then popped back up like a cork. If she didn't pull free of the creek, she wouldn't have to worry about a future with Liam.

Despite it being a midsummer day, the water chilled her to the bone, taking her breath away every time she went under. A slam against a jutting boulder spun her around. She reached up to grab a tree leaning over the water, only to be forced under again. It became harder and harder to keep her head above water.

God, help me.

Alisa swallowed a mouthful and coughed, swallowing more. She reached for a pine branch and held on. The water held her flat on the surface until she could no longer hold on, then slammed her against the bank.

She planted her feet against another large rock and grabbed the root of a tree protruding from the soil. Hand over hand, inch-by-inch, she pulled herself from the water, and lay like a dying fish as she gasped for air. She hadn't drowned. Alisa glanced heavenward. "Thank you."

Her prayer died on her lips as the very man Sheriff Westbrook sought stood over her.

"Well, I didn't expect this." Preston reached down and hauled her to her feet. "Where's the drive?"

"What drive?" She glanced around for a weapon or

a way to escape. Both ideas died as Jones limped into sight. "You look terrible. You need to see a doctor."

"As if that's going to happen." He clutched a gun in his right hand. "Thanks to you and rancher boy, I'd have to go to another state."

"The drive, Miss Gosling." Preston held out his hand.

With a sigh, Alisa pulled it from her pocket. "Good luck with it working after my dunking."

"You'd better hope it does. Let's go."

"I gave you the drive. Leave me here." She had no idea where she was anyway.

"No, you're better off as leverage." He gave her a shove.

She stumbled but righted herself, holding her right arm tight to her side. Now that she wasn't in danger of drowning, her side ached from the water bashing her against the rocks. A cough had her hissing against the pain.

"Are you injured?"

"As if you cared."

"Can't have you dying before you've served your purpose."

They stepped from the trees onto a dirt road where an older model truck waited. Alisa froze. If they forced her in the truck, she'd end up who knew where. "How did you know where I was?"

"We saw you fall in after Jones shot the cowboy." He opened the passenger side door. "Climb in."

She whirled to dash away.

The click of a gun stopped her.

"I'll shoot you," Jones said. "I'm not the gentleman Preston is."

"You'll follow orders," his boss growled. "Inside, Miss Gosling. The mud is ruining my Italian leather shoes. That makes me angry."

Alisa had no choice but to climb in the truck. Not an easy task with painful ribs, nor a fast one. From the breathing of the man behind her, she could tell he was growing frustrated with her.

Finally, she settled in the middle of the bench seat and soon found herself squeezed between Jones who smelled rank, and Preston who smelled of an expensive cologne. She pressed closer to the boss.

After forty-five minutes of driving, they pulled behind Preston's house. She bit back a smile. Alisa knew the perfect hiding place. Kingsley's safe could fit a small person like her and looked like part of the wall. The trick would be getting out of there without suffocating and/or letting Liam know where to find her.

Preston marched her to the house while Jones stored the car in a shed and out of sight. To anyone passing by, they'd think the house empty.

He led her to Kingsley's office where a laptop sat on top of his desk. "See if it works."

What if it didn't? Would he still keep her alive as a hostage? If he didn't see value in keeping her, she'd be killed, and she seriously doubted the thumb drive would work after being submerged in water for so long.

Thankfully, she was wrong. The list of names and account numbers showed on the screen. She stood from the chair and let Preston take her place.

"Have a seat where I can see you."

"I need to use the restroom."

"You're a big girl. Hold it until Jones can go with you."

She frowned. "What about privacy?"

"There isn't any." He bent over the keyboard and started typing. After a few minutes, his face darkened as he glanced her way. "This isn't the original. Where is the original?"

She swallowed against the lump stuck in her throat. "That's it."

"Miss Gosling." He leaned back and steepled his fingers. "The original was encrypted in a way that a copy wouldn't be. I'll ask you one more time. Where is the original?"

"With Sheriff Westbrook." Her shoulders slumped.

He stared at her for several intense seconds without blinking before speaking again. "Which means the feds have it. Looks like you'll be going to Europe, Miss Gosling. You're our ticket out of here. I'm going to assume your phone doesn't work after your swim." He pulled an old flip phone from a desk drawer and set it on the desk. "I need you to call the sheriff. Tell him to pull the feds back and give us access out of here. Do not stop us on the road or the airport. My plane will not be deterred from taking off or I'll leave your body on the tarmac. Understood?"

"Yes." Alisa cleared her throat and grabbed the phone. She didn't know Westbrook's private number so called the front desk and asked to be put through.

"Miss Gosling? Avery told us you fell in the creek. We've been searching for your body. Thank goodness, you're alive and well."

"I'm glad Avery is alive. I'm, uh, with Preston."

The line went silent, then Liam came on the line. "Repeat that."

"I'm with Preston. He knows the thumb drive I have

is fake, and in order not to kill me, he wants to leave Misty Hollow without being detained." She closed her eyes and leaned her head against the back of the chair. Exhaustion filled her. Pain riddled her body.

"Where are you? Are you hurt?"

She opened her eyes to the sight of Preston shaking his head and pointing a gun at her. "I can't tell you, and I think I might have a broken rib or two."

"Alisa—"

"If Preston's demands aren't met, he'll kill me." He probably would anyway, but every minute she still breathed gave her hope she'd find a way to escape.

Jones entered the room. "What's going on?"

"I'm out of here." Preston smiled, aiming his gun on Jones. "You're a liability now. Anyway, you'll be dead in a week from infection."

"Hold on," Alisa whispered, transfixed by the drama unfolding in front of her.

"No, I think you're mistaken." Jones gave an evil grin. "I'm taking your place."

Preston fired.

Jones doubled over but not before pulling off a shot of his own before crumbling to the ground.

Preston slumped over the desk, blood and brains splattered on the wall behind him.

"I'm at Kingsley's place. Jones and Preston just shot each other." Shock overtook her, and she trembled. "Come and get me, please." Tears welled in her eyes. It was finally over.

"On my way, sweetheart. Hold on. I'm coming with the sheriff and an ambulance."

Alisa hung up and set the phone back on the desk. Holding her side, she left the house and waited on the front porch, not wanting to be in the presence of death any longer than necessary. She lowered into a rocking chair and waited. Minutes later, she woke to Liam gently shaking her. "I fell in the creek and got knocked around."

Taking a deep breath, he put an arm around her and helped her to her feet. "I thought I'd lost you. When Avery told us he'd been shot and that you'd been taken down the creek, I thought I'd find your body on the bank somewhere."

"Instead, Preston found me." She took a shuddering breath as he helped her to the ambulance.

"Can you tell us what happened here?" The sheriff approached her.

"From what I could tell, Jones wanted to take over Preston's operation. So, Preston shot Jones, then Jones shot Preston. They're both dead in the office." She frowned. "It was far stranger than any movie I've ever seen. Anyway, the thumb drive had been encrypted. Preston knew it was a copy, but Jones didn't."

"You made a copy?" The sheriff frowned.

"I needed leverage. Good thing I had it, don't you think?" She groaned as the paramedic pressed on her side.

"I think it's just bruised, but the hospital will x-ray it just in case."

"I'll follow behind," Liam said. "I'm not letting you out of my sight again."

"Fine by me." Alisa smiled up at him. She had something she wanted to say once they were alone. "Let's watch the sun kiss the mist tomorrow."

"Absolutely." He kissed her and stepped back as the paramedics helped her onto a gurney, and the doors closed.

Epilogue

Alisa breathed deep of the morning air as the sun rose and lit the misty sky with hues of salmon and pumpkin. "I didn't think I'd have a chance to see this again." She leaned against Liam. "Or you."

"I have to admit the same thoughts crossed my mind." His arm tightened around her.

"I had hope when I climbed out of the water, then Preston and Jones arrived. They'd seen me fall in and followed the creek, checking every place I might climb out. Then, I thought for sure I wouldn't see you again. They were going to fly to Europe."

"Not even an ocean could keep us apart. I'd have followed." He straightened, setting her a bit away from him. "I have something for you." He pulled an envelope from the picnic basket and handed it to her.

"What is it?" she opened the flap.

"A deed."

"To what?" Her eyes widened.

"The little blue house. Mrs. Mayfield told me that owning a home was your dream."

"It was….once." Now, all she wanted was him. "Why?"

His eyes softened. "I'd hoped as a wedding gift." He

took her hands in his. "I love you more than the breath I take. More than that view." Liam smiled jerking his head toward where the mist dissipated. "Will you marry me?"

"We don't know each other that well. Not really." Her gaze stayed locked on his. She needed to know he really wanted to marry her and wasn't making a spur-of-the-moment decision. "That's your mother's house."

"She'd want the woman I love to have it for whatever purpose she wanted. Do you not love me, Alisa?" His features fell.

Tears trickled down her cheeks. "I do. With everything in me, but these circumstances—"

"Formed a bond that can't be broken." His grip on her hands tightened. "I know you, Alisa, and we have a lifetime to learn more about each other."

She studied the face she loved so much and decided the risk would be worth taking. "Yes, I'll marry you. I don't know when I fell in love, but you were all I could think about in that creek and after Preston grabbed me. Seeing you again was what I wanted."

"That makes me very happy." His voice grew husky as he leaned close and claimed her lips.

This one wasn't timid or quick. The steam from their last deep kiss was no comparison to the heat of this one. A kiss of belonging, of promises—the dispelling of fear and the hope of a future. Of belonging to each other.

Alisa had come home.

The End

Dear Reader,

I hoped you enjoyed your time in Misty Hollow. If you did, please leave a review and check out the other books in the Misty Hollow series. Also, stay tuned for the next book, Lethal Inheritance.

Cynthia Hickey

www.cynthiahickey.com

Multi-published and best-selling author, Cynthia Hickey, has taught writing at many conferences and small writing retreats. She and her husband run the publishing press, Winged Publications, which includes some of the CBA's best well-known authors. They live in Arizona and Arkansas, becoming snowbirds with two dogs and one cat. They have ten grandchildren who them busy and tell everyone they know that "Nana is a writer."

Connect with me on FaceBook
Twitter
Sign up for my newsletter and receive a free short story

www.cynthiahickey.com

Follow me on Amazon
And Bookbub

Enjoy other books by Cynthia Hickey

Misty Hollow
Secrets of Misty Hollow
Deceptive Peace
Calm Surface
Lightning Never Strikes Twice

The Tail Waggin' Mysteries
Cat-Eyed Witness
The Dog Who Found a Body
Troublesome Twosome
Four-Legged Suspect
Unwanted Christmas Guest
Wedding Day Cat Burglar

Brothers Steele
Sharp as Steele
Carved in Steele
Forged in Steele
Brothers Steele (All three in one)

The Brothers of Copper Pass
Wyatt's Warrant
Dirk's Defense
Stetson's Secret
Houston's Hope
Dallas's Dare
Seth's Sacrifice
Malcolm's Misunderstanding
The Brothers of Copper Pass Boxed Set

Time Travel
The Portal

Tiny House Mysteries
No Small Caper
Caper Goes Missing
Caper Finds a Clue

<u>Caper's Dark Adventure</u>
<u>A Strange Game for Caper</u>
<u>Caper Steals Christmas</u>
<u>Caper Finds a Treasure</u>
<u>Tiny House Mysteries boxed set</u>

Wife for Hire – Private Investigators
<u>Saving Sarah</u>
<u>Lesson for Lacey</u>
<u>Mission for Meghan</u>
<u>Long Way for Lainie</u>
<u>Aimed at Amy</u>
<u>Wife for Hire</u> (all five in one)

A Hollywood Murder
<u>Killer Pose, book 1</u>
<u>Killer Snapshot, book 2</u>
<u>Shoot to Kill, book 3</u>
<u>Kodak Kill Shot, book 4</u>
<u>To Snap a Killer</u>
<u>Hollywood Murder Mysteries</u>

Shady Acres Mysteries
<u>Beware the Orchids, book 1</u>
<u>Path to Nowhere</u>
<u>Poison Foliage</u>
<u>Poinsettia Madness</u>
<u>Deadly Greenhouse Gases</u>
<u>Vine Entrapment</u>
<u>Shady Acres Boxed Set</u>

CLEAN BUT GRITTY Romantic Suspense

Highland Springs

Murder Live
Say Bye to Mommy
To Breathe Again
Highland Springs Murders (all 3 in one)

Colors of Evil Series

Shades of Crimson
Coral Shadows

The Pretty Must Die Series

Ripped in Red, book 1
Pierced in Pink, book 2
Wounded in White, book 3
Worthy, The Complete Story

Lisa Paxton Mystery Series

Eenie Meenie Miny Mo
Jack Be Nimble
Hickory Dickory Dock
Boxed Set

Hearts of Courage
A Heart of Valor
The Game
Suspicious Minds
After the Storm

Local Betrayal
Hearts of Courage Boxed Set

Overcoming Evil series
Mistaken Assassin
Captured Innocence
Mountain of Fear
Exposure at Sea
A Secret to Die for
Collision Course
Romantic Suspense of 5 books in 1

INSPIRATIONAL

Nosy Neighbor Series
Anything For A Mystery, Book 1
A Killer Plot, Book 2
Skin Care Can Be Murder, Book 3
Death By Baking, Book 4
Jogging Is Bad For Your Health, Book 5
Poison Bubbles, Book 6
A Good Party Can Kill You, Book 7
Nosy Neighbor collection

Christmas with Stormi Nelson

The Summer Meadows Series
Fudge-Laced Felonies, Book 1
Candy-Coated Secrets, Book 2
Chocolate-Covered Crime, Book 3
Maui Macadamia Madness, Book 4

All four novels in one collection

The River Valley Mystery Series
Deadly Neighbors, Book 1
Advance Notice, Book 2
The Librarian's Last Chapter, Book 3
All three novels in one collection

Historical cozy
Hazel's Quest

Historical Romances
Runaway Sue
Taming the Sheriff
Sweet Apple Blossom
A Doctor's Agreement
A Lady Maid's Honor
A Touch of Sugar
Love Over Par
Heart of the Emerald
A Sketch of Gold
Her Lonely Heart

Finding Love the Harvey Girl Way
Cooking With Love
Guiding With Love
Serving With Love
Warring With Love
All 4 in 1

Finding Love in Disaster
The Rancher's Dilemma
The Teacher's Rescue
The Soldier's Redemption

Woman of courage Series

A Love For Delicious
Ruth's Redemption
Charity's Gold Rush
Mountain Redemption
They Call Her Mrs. Sheriff
Woman of Courage series

Short Story Westerns
Desert Rose
Desert Lilly
Desert Belle
Desert Daisy
Flowers of the Desert 4 in 1

Contemporary

Romance in Paradise
Maui Magic
Sunset Kisses
Deep Sea Love
3 in 1

Finding a Way Home
Service of Love

Hillbilly Cinderella
Unraveling Love
I'd Rather Kiss My Horse

Christmas
Dear Jillian
Romancing the Fabulous Cooper Brothers
Handcarved Christmas
The Payback Bride
Curtain Calls and Christmas Wishes
Christmas Gold
A Christmas Stamp
Snowflake Kisses
Merry's Secret Santa
A Christmas Deception

The Red Hat's Club (Contemporary novellas)

Finally
Suddenly
Surprisingly
The Red Hat's Club 3 – in 1

Short Story

One Hour **(A short story thriller)**
Whisper Sweet Nothings **(a Valentine short romance)**